THE BEST OF
GAMUT

THE BEST OF GAMUT

EDITED BY
RICHARD THOMAS

FOREWORD BY
PRIYA SHARMA

ROSLINDALE, MA

Published by Gamut, Inc., a Massachusetts charitable corporation with a principal place of business at 5 Bradford Circle, Roslindale, MA 02131.

The stories contained in this anthology are works of fiction. All incidents, situations, institutions, governments, and people are fictional and any similarity to characters or persons living or dead is strictly coincidental.

The Best of Gamut
Anthology Copyright © 2023 by Gamut, Inc.
Foreword © 2023 by Priya Sharma
Introduction Copyright © 2023 by Richard Thomas
Introduction Copyright © 2023 by R.B. Wood

Individual stories previously appeared in *Gamut Magazine* in 2017 and are copyrighted by their respective authors.

All rights reserved. No part of this book may be reproduced in any form or by any electronic or mechanical means, including information storage and retrieval systems, without permission in writing from the publisher, except in the case of short passages quoted in reviews.

First Trade Edition
January 2024

ISBN: 979-8-9892478-0-6
Library of Congress Control Number: 2023948175

Cover and Interior Illustrations by Luke Spooner | Carrion House
Designed by Todd Keisling | Dullington Design Co.

Manufactured in the United States of America

www.houseofgamut.com

TABLE OF CONTENTS

FOREWORD
  by Priya Sharma 7
INTRODUCTION
  by R.B. Wood 9
INTRODUCTION
  by Richard Thomas 13
ETCH THE UNTHINKABLE
  by Kurt Fawver 17
METAL, SEX, MONSTERS
  by Maria Haskins 25
SLIPPING PETALS FROM THEIR SKINS
  by Kristi DeMeester 31
THE GHOST STORIES WE TELL AROUND PHOTON FIRES
  by Cassandra Khaw 53
GARNIER
  by Brian Evenson 67
LOVE STORY, AN EXORCISM
  by Michelle E. Goldsmith 83
AN ENDING (ASCENT)
  by Michael Wehunt 97
THE BUBBLEGUM MAN
  by Eric Reitan 127

THE MARK
  by Kathryn E. McGee 143
FIGURE 8
  by E. Catherine Tobler 153
THE MOMENTS BETWEEN
  by Kate Jonez 171
THEY ARE PASSING BY WITHOUT TURNING
  by Helen Marshall 183
CRADLE LAKE
  by Jan Stinchcomb 205
THE ARROW OF TIME
  by Kate Dollarhyde 211
THE GOD OF LOW THINGS
  by Stephen Graham Jones 221
BIOGRAPHIES AND ENDNOTES 249
ACKNOWLEDGMENTS 261

FOREWORD

Priya Sharma

My abiding impression of Richard Thomas is not only his passion for stories but for nurturing storytellers. I was fortunate enough to be involved in a small way in Storyville, his virtual writing school, and what struck me the most was that he didn't just want to teach skills and techniques. He wanted more. For each writer to find what was unique within them, and to help them voice it.

I see *Gamut* as an extension of this philosophy. *Gamut* was launched in 2017 on Kickstarter, describing itself as neo-noir speculative literary fiction. If that seems like a broad banner, it is. It accepted everything from thrillers to bizarro. I think the crucial part of its guidelines was this:

You know that part of your writing that you question—that is weird and doesn't fit neatly into genre or a mold? Write more of that please.

I applaud this. The work that falls down the cracks,

that we're reluctant to reveal, is often the bravest, the most innovative, or interesting. Bravo to *Gamut* for actively encouraging writers to submit them.

There are certainly things here that you'll recognize (side shows, nocturnal visitations, clones, cyberpunk ghosts in the machine, possession, time travel and infestation, for example) but none of it is generic. The unifier is the same base-note of an existence that's off-kilter.

I'm not interested in remarkable people in fiction. Everyone is remarkable when you scratch the surface. What I want to read about is what people do in the face of the remarkable and the unfathomable. This is what excites me about genre fiction, and all those stories that don't fit in tidy niches. I enjoy clever ideas in fiction, but I also want to feel, not just think. The stories in *Gamut* ask questions about the human experience—sibling love and loss, the pursuit of beauty or immortality, infidelity, abuse, loneliness, our very identity itself. *What do we do in the face of the unthinkable that is death? What makes us unique as human beings if it's not our DNA? What happens when you're a child and you're terrified of your best friend? And finally, hilariously, weirdly, and tragically—what do you do when you hit a prairie dog on the way over to your girlfriend's house?*

As *Gamut* magazine relaunches, I sincerely hope it continues to mine this vein of the strange, and that there will be more of these wonderful stories to come.

—Priya Sharma
Wirral, Merseyside
United Kingdom
July 10th, 2023

INTRODUCTION
R. B. Wood

I remember my son saying to me, in a voice of whispered and sincere pleading, "I wish magic were real!" This was a few decades ago when he was seven or eight, and I'd just closed the book I'd finished reading to him before bed. I smiled at him and said, "When I was reading to you, did you see in your mind the dragons and the knights and the wizards of the story?"

"Oh yes, Dad! I could see them all!"

"Well, then you experienced a kind of magic, didn't you? You traveled to another world, my son. So, in a sense, that *was* real magic. *Story* magic!"

He's been an avid reader ever since.

Magic is all around us. We only must look for it. I've survived two encounters with cancer that statistics and mathematics would have made you believe were both death sentences. Magic, miracle, or science? Depending on who you ask, the answer you might get would be very different.

But there are other types of magic, too—the magic that can happen when you connect with your soul mate or when you work with the perfect group of people. They are not perfect people. I mean a group of people that are perfect together.

When *Gamut* magazine began, magic struck. The perfect people who shared a love of dark fiction and wanted to share that with the world. Unfortunately, for other reasons, the business could not go into a second year in a sustainable way, so *Gamut*, as it was, folded.

But the magic that was *Gamut* would live on. And you hold the "Best of" that first year in your hands now. This anthology is the perfect end to the first chapter of *Gamut*. Now on to chapter two!

In 2023, *Gamut* turned the page to become the House of Gamut, the home of dark speculative fiction. Not only will the magazine return in 2024—but we will be opening a publishing house and an eLearning academy for readers and burgeoning authors who want to learn more about the magical art of writing. We have incorporated as a non-profit, and will be opening for donations soon enough. These monies will help cover the professional rates we will be paying our artists, but, more importantly, we will be able to subsidize magazine subscription costs, costs for books from our publishing house, and the costs for classes for underrepresented and underprivileged students who want to tell their stories. That is our goal.

INTRODUCTION

If we do it right, the possibilities are endless—because I think everyone should be able to share their own kind of magic with the world. Don't you?

—Richard Wood
Boston, MA
September 15th, 2023

INTRODUCTION

Richard Thomas

I'm so glad you're back here with us at *Gamut* magazine, for this anthology focusing on some of the best new stories we published back in 2017. We're really excited about the future of the House of Gamut—the magazine, the publishing house, and the teaching academy. But the question that may be on your lips right now is how did we select the stories for *The Best of Gamut?* Here are a few answers.

The first thing I did was to reach out to my editors at the original *Gamut* magazine—Mercedes Yardley, Dino Parenti, and Casey Frechette. I asked each of them to send over their four favorite stories, and that's what they did. There was some overlap, of course, and so we didn't have 16 in total, but much less. I went back and looked at the original submissions—and there were five stories that got "yes" votes from ALL of us (out of over 50 new submissions) so those seemed like mandatory stories to include. When I re-read them (re-reading ALL of the selections here) I agreed. After that, we took a look at the stories that were long-listed by Ellen Datlow for *The Best Horror of the Year* anthology—there were quite a few. And then it just came down to a few stories and authors that were favorites of mine. It's all subjective, right?

Included in here is a wide range of fiction—a gamut of human emotions you might say. There is fantasy, science fiction, and horror. There is old weird and new-weird. There are clowns and monsters, clones and spiders, existential dread and buried secrets, time travel and even a few prairie dogs. What these stories (and authors) have in common is that each and every one of them stood out, amazed me, moved me, and blew my mind. I hope that you enjoy each and every story in here.

At the House of Gamut we are looking forward to publishing a wide range of dark speculative fiction for many years to come, and we hope you'll come along for the ride.

—Richard Thomas
Chicago, IL
September 12th, 2023

THE BEST OF
GAMUT

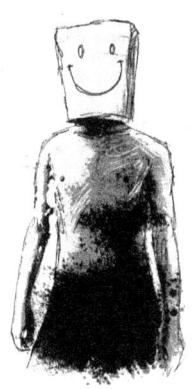

ETCH THE UNTHINKABLE

Kurt Fawver

The theater was located in a long-abandoned warehouse on the outskirts of the city. Roof partially collapsed, windows mostly broken, and walls covered in thick, dark mounds of unidentifiable lichen and fungus, it seemed an unlikely place for a comedy show. And yet, despite this unlikelihood (or maybe because of it), the queue to enter stretched halfway around the moldering structure.

Every person who waited in line held two items: a rusted token with a pair of falcon wings imprinted on both sides and a one-gallon container filled with gasoline. These would-be patrons chatted with one another in brief, excited blurbs, their eyes glistening with desperate hope. A great deal of nervous laughter punctuated the evening sky and phrases such as "I always thought Etch was an urban legend," "Do you think he can do it?" and "Can a clown really be *that* funny?" floated up from the murmuring throng.

As dusk retreated before night's swift blade, the warehouse doors swung open and the conversations quieted to barely whispered confessions and epithets. Gravity pulled harder and a litany of scourges filled the air. "Cancer," "Alzheimer's," "ALS," "depression": these were the words that suddenly crowded out the laughter and anticipation that had hung like colorful balloons above the old industrial building only moments before; they strangled the firmament and burst every floating joy to make room for themselves. Even the very stars above began to ache and roil with diseased sufferings.

The line began to inch forward.

Movement made what lay within the warehouse more than possibility, more than dream. It meant that Etch would perform. It meant that everything told in fables and fairy tales might be true. It meant that monsters did, indeed, hide under the bed and inside the closet.

When the audience began to shuffle toward the entrance, many people peeled off into the night, rushing back to their cars, their homes, their families. Later, palms still sweaty, legs still shaking, they'd face the same infirmities that drove them to seek out the show in the first place and they'd reconsider their decision. They'd claw and they'd scrape and they'd try to win their battles on their own, but, inevitably, they would be overrun by the insatiable masses that had accumulated within them. To their last breath, these stragglers would try to imagine, in vain, what it might have been like to be in Etch's gallery and partake of his show. Eyes sunken and muscles withered, they'd try to picture themselves inside the makeshift theater. They'd try to conjure the jokes and skits and pratfalls, but none would be right. They'd dream of Etch's face, but Etch had no face like they'd ever seen. They'd think often of the others, the ones who'd gone on without them, who'd chanced the meeting with Etch. When their time came, it is true that they would die in as much safety as death can afford: in their own beds, with their families nearby, without sensation and without illumination. And yet, even so, even in their placid demises, they would remain discontented and ever-wondering for reasons they understood too well.

Such was the future of those who broke from the line.

The people who remained, however, discovered an entirely different fate. Hands trembling and legs weak, they passed into the warehouse where a pair of naked doormen greeted their arrival. The doormen, unclothed but for paper bags with smiley faces drawn upon them that they wore over their heads, collected the tokens from the entrants and directed them to a series of patio tables and rickety plastic chairs. Here the audience members waited in silence. No one dared speak, for speech would have invited recognition and in this place no one wanted to be acknowledged for the choice they'd made.

Instead, all sets of eyes were pasted to the center of the abandoned warehouse floor, upon which stretched a wide, ramshackle stage composed of loose wooden planks arranged atop a series of sawhorses. Two poles stood at either end of the stage, with a clothesline strung between them. On the taut line hung a wide swath of red velvet with a strange helical sigil stitched across its surface. The entire panorama was lit by two candelabras set at opposing sides of the makeshift curtain.

Once everyone in the audience had slid into their seats, the bagmen-ushers closed the doors and chained them shut, clicking in place a series of heavy padlocks so that further entrance—or exit—would be impossible. The anticipation in the room swelled, and so too did a tang of sweat spread throughout the warehouse, its scent growing sharp and unforgiving as a surgeon's scalpel.

After what seemed like several lifetimes, a figure emerged from under the curtain. A round, noseless face, glowing pale in the guttering light. Unpainted, diamond-shaped eyes without irises, dark as the edge of the universe. A toothless, frozen grin, too wide, much too wide, ringed not in red but in a shimmering, nameless color almost beyond human ken. And, within a black and white polka dotted jumpsuit, joints, too many joints, all bending at uncanny, marionette angles.

Etch the Clown. Etch the Unthinkable.

In silence, the audience stirred, recoiled. They'd not anticipated this *thing*, not even with all the legends they'd heard, the midnight tales told over campfires and crackling hearths. Fear rolled over the warehouse. Someone stood and knocked over a table, which rattled against the floor.

Etch cocked his head to the side, grin unwavering, eyes unblinking. His body contorted like a spider about to leap upon its prey.

A chair squealed against cement as it was pushed back. The audience tensed, most readying for flight.

But Etch did not leap from his stage. Instead, he folded in upon himself, an impossible Gordian knot of limbs and rolled to one side of the stage, then unfolded and stood. He gazed upon his audience, his head again cocked to the side and performed what could only be called a grotesque jig.

In the audience, muscles ached. Hands trembled. Flight was still a very real possibility. Fear was still heavy in the atmosphere.

And then, from a distant world on the outskirts of sanity and reason, a laugh—the first drop of rain from an impending hurricane.

One laugh grew to two, two to four, and four to eight. Soon, every member of the audience rocked in their seats, on their feet, on the floor. They couldn't understand why they laughed. If they thought about it—and thought was becoming ever more difficult—they could find no real trigger for their laughter other than Etch's horrifying jig. Yet they couldn't contain it. In truth, they didn't want to contain it. And so laughter swept through the warehouse, shook its foundations; it tore at the sinews of throats, at the linings of lungs, drowning every care, every thought, every emotion.

Etch again folded in upon himself, rolled to the opposite end of the stage, unfolded and danced.

The laughter grew more unhinged, less the noise from an audience than a madhouse.

Etch watched, head tilted, eyes unblinking, grin always too wide.

On and on it went. Etch becoming infinitely recursive,

performing his macabre dance at one end of the stage then the other, and the people in the audience laughing louder, laughing as they never had, so hard, so long, without so much reason.

The laughter did not stop, could not stop. It continued to grow wildly, all out of proportion to the vessels through which it flowed. It strained bodies to their breaking points, blotting out pain and horror with a maniacal glee. It crashed through flesh, through minds, consuming all in its path. Jaws cracked and splintered. Larynges shredded like tissue paper. Lungs burst. Hearts sputtered and stopped.

One by one, the members of the audience surrendered to the insatiable laughter and slipped away into the absurdity of it all, blood foaming from their gaping smiles. One by one, they dropped to the floor or slouched cold and limp in their seats.

Gradually, the volume diminished and Etch ceased his metronome motion. He stood at the head of a satisfied crowd, his inscrutable grin never wavering, his eyes ever impassive and searching.

When, near dawn, stillness and silence fell final, the bagmen ushers grabbed the gasoline containers that sat atop every table and poured their contents over the audience. They flipped the candelabras onto the warehouse floor, mounted the stage, and linked arms with Etch, whose arachnid reach drew them to himself, into himself, through himself. A point of searing white light formed at his chest and he squeezed the bagmen into it, their forms impossibly stretched and flattened like wet clay.

Flames quickly overtook the warehouse.

The stage began to burn, Etch's backdrop going up like a phoenix eager for rebirth.

His grin still implacable, insatiable, Etch bowed to the dead room, then contorted and folded himself into the bright point at the center of his chest, disappearing into the harsh luster.

The flames roared in applause.

The show had ended.

The laughter, however, would go ever, ever on.

METAL, SEX, MONSTERS
Maria Haskins

Yes, officer: I do remember my first time. I was thirteen, and the room smelled of drugstore perfume, apple-scented shampoo, and sticky lip gloss. I remember what the boy tasted like, too: potato chips and popcorn, teenage sweat, and bated breath. It was in the basement of a friend's house, a party, out of sight of the parents, and Judas Priest was playing on the stereo when someone turned off the lights and said we were playing a kissing game: everyone had to walk around in the dark and kiss whoever they could get a hold of. It sounds kind of louche now, I guess, but it was 1981, and it's not like we were drinking anything but soft drinks mixed with lemonade.

The boy's hair and eyes were brown and I'd had a crush on him since grade two, though I'd never considered doing anything about it. I'd never kissed anyone before, either. But in the dark, with Rob Halford screaming about working class frustration in Margaret Thatcher's Britain, he grabbed hold of me, probably out of pity, and kissed me.

I liked kissing him: liked the rush of blood to my head and groin, liked the way he held me. He might have tried to pull away soon after, or maybe he was just trying to breathe, but I persisted and he acquiesced, and when his lips parted just a little, I kissed harder, penetrating his wet, warm mouth with my tongue, nipping at the flesh. There was a taste then, familiar and new at the same time, slipping through me, of salt like tears, of rusted iron and oxidized copper.

I probed and bit and licked as something shuddered awake deep beneath my skin, rippling like the surface of a submerged dream, its sudden heat radiating through my capillaries, burning through my eyes and fingers, blistering my lips and cheeks.

Will you look at that? Look at my hands. Even now, thirty-five years later, the memory of it makes me tremble.

No, officer. I pulled away. He caught his breath and I thought he'd scream, thought he'd tell everyone that I had bit him. The blood was there to prove it, on his lips and chin, on my tongue as I swallowed. But he just put his hand to his mouth and looked at me, as if he'd caught a sideways glimpse of the hunger lurking inside me.

His family moved away later that summer. Probably just as well, even though I missed him.

But that's not what you want me to talk about. You brought police photographs.

Let me see. Yes, they were all mine. Such gorgeous boys.

Hell-bent for leather, wouldn't you say, each and every one? But then, rock and heavy metal gigs have been my venues of choice from the start. I love the music, of course, always have, and I figured those places were good for hiding in plain sight. There, I was just another hungry groupie, just another starving fangirl jonesing for a fix: unremarkable, disposable, forgettable. Considering how long it's taken you to find me, I guess I was right about that. But it's the bodies I love most of all. That's what kept me coming back. All that lovely flesh wrapped in sweat and studs and tight denim, bones reverberating with the amplified sound of guitars and drums and bass, shouted vocals clawing at their throats, the air thrumming with scent, everyone resplendent in eyeliner and hairspray, lace and Spandex. All those beautiful people: souls loosening their grip on mortal coils, words and breaths and hands rising, each one wanting to taste blood and skin, wanting to disappear into another, to be devoured by the music and the crowd…

No, officer. I don't need anything to drink. I just need a moment.

The second boy I kissed was the first one who went all the way. I waited for him in the shadows on a street corner, after the club had closed: I was eighteen and starving. I wonder if you've ever been as hungry. Maybe you have. I'd been good for so many years after that night in the basement. It was hard, but school's important, and besides, it takes more than hunger. At least for me. Something has to turn me on, there has to be a spark—heat, lust, love—call it what you want, but if I don't want them, if they don't want me, it's no good at all.

Sorry. You look uncomfortable. Is that too much information? But then that's what you want, isn't it? Information. That's what you said when you brought me here.

But I was telling you about the second boy.

Inside the club he'd slipped his arm around my waist and I'd left it there. He was barely older than I was, all strut and swagger in his leather jacket when he followed me outside and offered me a ride on his motorcycle. I held on to him, speeding through that gossamer night, my body bursting, flaring at the seams and joints with heat and hunger, trying not to take him too soon, too quick, trying to make it last.

In the tall grass by the river he took off my bra and I took him into me, whole and screaming and unwilling. He was my first, and I wasn't as gentle as I should have been, as I've learned to be since. But that mingled taste of him—leather, beer, and cigarettes—it whets my appetite even now, just thinking about how he scraped and rubbed against my viscera as I brought him deep inside of me.

That was a long time ago. I've devoured so many boys and men since then.

How many? I couldn't tell you. I've not counted them. But, yes. More than in your photographs, certainly. If I wanted them, and they wanted me, then I took them. And when I reached out, when I opened up, and they saw me in my glory, when they were blinded by my bliss and consumed—they were not afraid. Not in the end, at least.

Are you afraid, officer? Or is that too personal a question to ask?

What it's like? Why would you ask me that? You said you have video footage, so you must know. I don't know what it's like from outside. I only know what it feels like from within.

...heat and light, ignited and extinguished in the same moment

...reaching out through flesh and bones and web of veins and skeins of nerves

...unfurling myself

...unleashing myself

...unhinging myself

...unmaking them

...savouring the quavering tissue of life and memories, their first and last flashes of pain and ecstasy, the moment of their birth and the instant of their death.

Afterward, I can still feel them inside me for a while: plucking them like strings to hear the whispered echoes of who they were.

Yes, thank you, officer. I do need something to drink now.

What I am? Don't ask me that. Tell me what you see, instead, when you look at me.

I don't know what I am. I don't know what awoke in that basement when I was thirteen, with British Steel pounding beneath my flesh, blood riveted to my tongue; when I awoke and knew that I was no longer what I'd thought I was, that I wore the body I'd thought was mine like a second skin pulled tight over my true self.

I've thought about that kiss, that boy, every day since.

Something was different that time. I know that now. I sensed it, but didn't understand it until later, maybe not until tonight. That he was like me. That he hungered, too.

I wonder if he's looked for me like I've looked for him.

I'd know him anywhere. I'd know his dark brown eyes, would know his hair even if it's thinner and streaked with grey, would know the scent of him even thirty-five years on. I'd know him no matter where I saw him, or what uniform or badge he wore.

I'd know the heat, radiating from his skin before we even touched.

Yes, officer. I would know you, even if I'd waited decades, trapped and lonely inside an aging husk of skin and flesh, even if I'd lingered, sleepless for a million years in an empty space of stars and quantum rifts. I'd still know you.

Do you remember it? The dizzying taste of me in you? The fleeting promise of it on your tongue? Of course you do. That's why you brought me to this bar rather than the police station.

And if we kissed again, you and I, here and now, with this Judas Priest song cutting through us like a screaming metal blade, cutting all our memories open; with the noise and blood and hunger throbbing in us like when we were thirteen; if we kissed now, what would we become then, you and I, if we unfurled, unhinged, unleashed ourselves together—devouring each other, our light and heat bleeding into the other, pulsing, flowing, mingling, fusing into one?

What, I wonder, will we become, now?

SLIPPING PETALS FROM THEIR SKINS

Kristi DeMeester

Carolina smells of viburnum when we bury her. My sister and I stand over the closed casket and pretend the fetid, cloying scent is the death lilies wreathed about the church, but of course we know better. Know if we opened up the box we'd put her in and pried open her mouth, those tiny white flowers would peek out from her throat like lace against her teeth.

One by one, the mourners file past, their hands against our shoulders, our cheeks, and we thank them for coming. Yes, she was a beautiful girl. Yes, we would miss her very much.

Mama is still in the front pew and hasn't moved since the minister got up and started the prayer, so it's up to Nettie and me to deal with all of the people who came.

"God will see you through, Mackenzie. Trust in his will,"

Pastor Mills says, as he lays a heavy hand on my shoulder, kneading at the muscle there. He means it to be comforting, but I can feel his sympathy already dissolving, a fleeting mask of grief.

When the church finally empties out, I have blisters from the new shoes Mama bought me. Mama still hasn't moved. She clutches the yellowed handkerchief Daddy left when he passed, but that was a long time ago, when we were just babies. I never knew how to mourn him. I feel bad for Mama, but I only know how to mourn Carolina, and I'm pretty sure Nettie feels the same way. Can't miss the things you never knew you were supposed to.

Mama's eyes are dry when we go to her, but they fix on some far away point, and she lets us help her up, our arms wrapped around her waist.

"Let's go," I say. Nettie and I balance Mama between us and leave Carolina behind in her cramped, cold box as we make our way to the cemetery behind the church.

In less than an hour, Carolina is in the ground. Nettie and I throw dirt into the hole while the preacher mumbles a prayer, and then the men from the church join together to fill it. A shower of stones to keep our sister buried. I want to tell them it won't hold her there, but it wouldn't change anything. Carolina told me.

The preacher's words finally dry up, and he looks at all of us, all of his lambs, with eyes like a beat dog and tells us to look to God when we are in the dark valley.

It's dark by the time we get home, the house a smaller shadow among the oak trees planted out front and the deep woods on both sides of the house. Mama goes straight to her bedroom. The lock clicks behind her, and Nettie looks at me.

"Reckon she knows? About Carolina? What really happened, and she's coming back?"

"Not right now, Nettie. I'm tired. Give it a rest, okay?"

My sister frowns, pulls a strand of raven dark hair in front of her face and sticks the ends into her mouth. "But she's coming back, right?"

The same old song and dance. The same old question. I'm tired of hearing Nettie ask it.

Outside, the night air beats against the house with frozen fingers; it settles around all the doors and windows, and tries to claw its way inside.

It was Carolina who let in whatever was tapping on the pane outside our bedroom. The windows were cracked to let in the July evening air so we wouldn't stifle in our beds. It was Carolina who rose and went to the window and saw the beautiful thing moving through the night. Carolina who heard the voices coming from under the ground and followed them into something we could never understand. Four months have passed since the first night Carolina changed, and I still don't understand. Not completely.

It doesn't matter how it rattles at the windows or shakes the door, I'm not letting it inside. Even if what it brings is something so beautiful it makes you ache.

"Leave it alone, Nettie."

"But why would she—"

"I said leave it alone!" I whirl on my sister, my palm itching with the need to crack her across her mulish face, and she scuttles backward, her eyes all scrunched up.

Truth is, I don't know why Carolina did it either. Why she opened the window and breathed in whatever lingered in the air, why she gobbled up that terrible, beautiful thing until it came leaking out of her in sweetly scented petals and green vines.

At first, it didn't hurt her. She plucked the profusion of stems and petals from her skin and left them scattered around the house, or bunched in vases. Daisies and tulips the color of early spring on the kitchen table, or a single pansy tucked in her hair. Mama never questioned where they came from, and Carolina never let Mama see what was happening to her, and we all giggled whenever Carolina showed us the newest blooming. Three sisters hiding a secret.

She started bleeding in late November. Slick crimson and algae-colored liquid dribbled from her lips when she tried to speak, and there were mornings she couldn't move.

"It's sucking everything out of me. Making room for something else," she said, and I held her hand while she looked up at me with eyes glittering with fever.

I told Mama that Carolina was sick and needed to stay home, and Carolina would wipe her mouth on the inside of her sheets when Mama came in to kiss her goodbye. Two weeks later, she was gone.

Nettie doesn't talk to me for the rest of the night, and Mama doesn't come out of her room. Every now and then I can hear her breath hitching, a slight choking sound, and then everything falls quiet again. Four times I walk to her door, put my hand on the doorknob and then take it off. I could go inside and lie to her. Tell her everything is going to be okay. Tell her Carolina is in a better place. But the lies sit bitter on my tongue, and I gulp air and hold it inside of me until I see pinpricks of light dancing at the edges of my vision.

Mama didn't want everyone coming over to the house after the funeral, bringing casseroles and funeral grits by the pound, and so I make a dinner out of a couple of American cheese slices and some pickle chips I find in the refrigerator. Nettie has retreated to our bedroom. I'm not sure if she's eaten or not, but she's twelve years old now and can figure it out for her own damn self.

Carolina was the one who would cook for us on nights when Mama was working late or didn't want to sit down at the kitchen table and pretend she understood us.

Seventeen and already talented in the kitchen, Carolina had a way of making whatever we had in the pantry match up just right with whatever meat or vegetable was in the fridge, and we wolfed her meals down while they were still too hot and scalded our tongues.

She tried to show me what to do. How to chop and mix

and add salt in just the right amounts, but I never caught on, burning more than I ever put on the table.

"It'll be your turn to take care of Nettie when I leave, Mack. You should know how to cook a little something by now. Jesus tap-dancing Christ, you're fifteen years old and barely know how to burn toast," she'd say, and swat at my butt with a kitchen towel.

I pad down the hallway to the only other bedroom besides Mama's. The bedroom we've shared our entire lives.

Carolina's bed is still tucked in the corner, her CD covers for Nirvana and pictures of the three of us still taped to the wall.

"I don't want to take her stuff down. I don't want to put it away. Like she was never here," Nettie says. She's buried under her ratty yellow comforter, a stuffed bear tucked beside her.

I pick my way across our bedroom, stepping over piles of clothes and scattered magazines, and sit on her mattress. It sags beneath me, and her body rolls toward mine. She wriggles away so she doesn't touch me.

"Look, I'm sorry okay? I don't want to take her stuff down either. It would be…weird."

She doesn't move out from under the blanket, and her voice sounds all hollowed out like she's talking to me from some deep, underground space.

"You think it'll be tonight? That she'll come back tonight? It isn't too soon, right? You don't think it's too soon?"

I don't want to turn and look at the window, at the slatted dark pouring through the blinds, but I do. There's nothing there. I'm not sure if I'm relieved or disappointed. Maybe a little bit of both.

"I don't know," I tell Nettie because I'm not sure what's going to happen next.

The night before her body went cold, Carolina crept into my bed and spooned herself against my back. Her skin was hot, burning with fever, and her breath smelled of metal and something decayed.

"It takes a while to become something beautiful. Time and cold, cold earth."

I turned to face her, and even in the dark, I could make out the purpled circles under her eyes. "What if you don't come back?" I asked her, and she kissed my forehead.

"You'll see. Be sure to leave the window open. Promise me," she said and extended her pinky.

I wrapped my own around it and promised her. Promised my sister I would help when she came back.

The next morning, she was gone. A violet—all dusk and cream—poked out of the center of her chest. Before Mama came in and saw her, I plucked the bloom from her skin, and crushed it in my palm. Later, I carried the violet out behind the house and buried it as far and as deep as I could.

"Be sure to leave the window open," Carolina had told me, but the window is closed. I don't think I'll be able to open it. Don't think I'll be able to keep my promise.

"Can you sleep here? With me? Just for tonight?" Nettie asks and pulls back the covers.

"Sure."

I climb in next to her, and her hair smells like her shampoo. Watermelon. Sweet in a way flowers aren't.

I'm beginning to drowse when the first sound comes. A scratching somewhere just beyond the walls. Like something trapped outside is trying to get in out of the cold.

Nettie sleeps on, her breathing regular and even, and I hold myself still, tense every muscle so whatever's at the window can't see me or feel me moving. Another round of scratching, and then the smell of freesias leaks into the room. Then the smell of lilacs and roses and jasmine and the delicate laced petals of peonies. A smell for summer nights and not the dead of winter.

When the tapping begins, the window rattling in its pane, Nettie starts. Immediately, she struggles to sit up, to turn to the window, but I wrap an arm around her and hold her down. "Shhh," I say, and she thrashes, the bedsheets tangling around our legs.

"Let me up, Mack, or I swear to God, I'll kick your ass."

The tapping is louder now, more insistent.

"It's her," Nettie says.

I clamp my hand over her mouth, and she bites me, her little teeth sinking into the soft pad of flesh between my thumb and forefinger. I shriek and let her go.

The tapping stops, and Nettie sits up, whipping to face the window.

"Why didn't you leave it open? Why would you do that?" she says.

Before I can grab her she's out of bed and running for the window.

"We don't know what it is," I say, but she doesn't listen.

She presses her face to the glass, her breath a white halo, and stares out into the dark night.

"Mack," she whispers, her voice thick with fear, and I don't want to go to her, don't want to see what's just outside of the window. "Mack, please," she says again, and my feet swing out, the wood floor freezing, and I make my way to my sister.

"What is she doing?" Nettie says, and I join her at the glass and stare out into the yard.

Carolina is on all fours, her hair pushed forward so it covers her face, and she creeps over the ground. Her hands stretch out before her, the fingers twitching as if she's teasing out what's in front of her. As if she can't see.

Dark roots or vines trail behind her, and they too twitch and shift. Once, one of the tendrils plunges into the dirt, and Carolina goes still, but it doesn't stay submerged, and she resumes her slow movement.

Nettie lifts her hand and brings it to the window as if she's going to knock. My heart jumps into my throat, but she only presses her palm against the glass.. Her other hand reaches for mine, so I wrap my fingers through hers, and together we watch our sister creep through the yard.

She never looks up at us, but I think she knows we are

there. A couple of times she lifts her head in our direction, and Nettie goes stiff against me, but then she swivels back to the dirt, and it's like all the air has been sucked out of the room and what's left is the smell of flowers.

We stand in front of the window until the sky turns early morning gray. When the first light hits her, Carolina crawls into the trees, and the fallen leaves and pine straw swallow her up. I want to call to her, to tell her to come back, that I'll open the window, but Nettie's hand is still in mine, and I bite down on everything I think I want to say.

"Come on. We have to get ready for school," I say, and Nettie walks out of the room without looking back.

Mama doesn't come out of her room while I pour bowls of cereal. We both pretend to eat, moving the soggy flakes around in the chipped, porcelain dishes, and then dump what's left into the garbage.

When Nettie's bus pulls up, gravel and dust flying, she trudges toward it. Before she gets on, she looks back at me, and for just a second her eyes look like Carolina's, and then the doors close, and the bus pulls away.

My own bus is late, and I make my way to the back and sit with my hood up, watching the landscape bleed past me. I fall asleep in first period. Ms. Volman's playing an audio book for us like she does every day and sitting her lazy ass behind her computer while she types away at some shitty poem she's writing. Sometimes I wonder how she got this job.

I dream of ranunculus, of verbena, of creeping phlox, and lily of the valley. Dream of Carolina guiding my hand over the identification book she found in the library, the strange syllables heavy on my tongue as we memorized the things growing from her skin. The air poisoned with the sweet, heady smell of her hair and breath, and she lifts her shirt to show me the place where the thorns have come through, the dried blood flecking against pale flesh. There's blood in her mouth, but she is still talking to me, crimson gore against her teeth as she smiles and tells me it's so much nicer under the ground.

I wake up when the bell rings with a cold fear in my belly. Drool pools under my cheek, and I wipe my face, gather my books, and hurry to second period.

I don't fall asleep again.

I'm the first one to get home, so I let myself in with the key I keep in my purse.

"Mama?" I call out into the quiet house. She doesn't answer me.

One by one, I tiptoe through the rooms, hold my breath each time I put my foot down, but each room is empty, and the dust sneaks past my lips and into my lungs. I pause outside of her bedroom and press my ear to the door.

At first there is no sound, but then I hear it. The slight hitching of her breath. She's crying again. I think of knocking, think of going in and wrapping my arms around her, but I'm not sure I would know how to do it, so I head back into the kitchen, pour myself a glass of milk, and carry it into the living room.

When Nettie comes home, she drops her backpack by the door and heads straight to the kitchen. There's the sound of a cabinet opening and closing, the rush of water running from the tap, and then she comes out of the kitchen and hurries past without a backward glance.

She's by the window fiddling with the latch when I go into the bedroom.

"What are you doing?" I ask her, and she jumps, turns from the window with guilt smeared across her face.

"Nothing," she says, but she angles her body away from me so I can't see what she's hidden in her hands.

She fights me when I grab at her hands and force them open, but eventually she sags, lets her arms drop to her sides, and what she's holding clatters to the floor.

A bottle of water and a small, thin saucer. Nettie looks away.

"What are you doing?" I ask.

"I thought if she was thirsty, she would come to the window."

"Nettie, you can't do this. We don't know what we saw last night. We were tired. A lot of shit's happened."

"I know what I saw, and so do you. Did you dream about her today, Mack? Did you dream about her like I did? Because I bet you did. I bet she came to you, too."

"It doesn't matter if I did or I didn't. We don't know what it is we would be inviting in. Carolina didn't know, and it messed everything up, Nettie, and now she's dead, and everything's fucked, and Mama won't even come out of her room. We can't let it in. Even if we think it's her. We can't."

"You told her you wouldn't leave her. You promised," Nettie says.

"We can't," I say, but the words are dead husks of everything buried deep down inside of me.

Nettie frowns and bends to grab the saucer. She stands and flings it against the far wall where it shatters. "Go to hell, Mack," she says and runs out of the room.

The front door slams, and I know I won't see Nettie for the rest of the afternoon. She'll come home when it's dark. Until then, I'm stuck in this house with the artifacts of my sister's life and a mother who's forgotten how to exist.

I stand in front of Carolina's bed and trace my fingertips over her lilac-c--olored quilt. She used to joke that one morning she would wake up and I wouldn't be able to tell where the petals left off and the quilt began. Nothing more than bone ground down into something lovely and fragrant.

Her dirty laundry is still piled on the floor, her boots still at the foot of her bed, the laces unraveled and spilling over the fake, worn leather. For a moment, I can see her sitting on the edge of the bed, bending over to lace them up, her face bright and smiling.

As quickly as the vision comes, it's gone, and I'm alone in the room. I pick up the bottle of water and the pieces of saucer I can find and carry them to the kitchen, put what's left of the saucer in the trash and pour the water down the sink.

I spend the afternoon staring at my math homework, but the numbers blur together, and I can't focus. Mama never comes out of her room, and the house is heavy with the silence of the dead.

I heat up a can of soup and pick out the noodles. Nettie still hasn't come home, and I go to the front door, open it, and look out into the yard. The sky is painted with dark purples and girlish pinks. Floral. A bridal bouquet of a sky.

Nettie isn't in the yard, and I watch the trees. My sister doesn't emerge from that dark space, so I stand in the doorway until my fingers are numb, as shadows steal into and swallow the oil-slicked colors of the sky.

I close the door but leave it unlocked. Nettie will come back. She *has to* come back.

I've only just closed my eyes when I hear the front door open. I sit up and wait for Nettie to come into the room, but other than the door opening, there are no other sounds. No shuffling footsteps coming down the hallway. Nothing.

"Nettie?" I call out into the void, but no response comes back.

My mouth floods with the taste of something sour, and my heart beats panic against my chest.

I walk slowly, pass Mama's still closed door, like the door to a tomb. Behind the wood, I wonder if Mama has stopped breathing. If her body has gone cold, too.

I pass the empty kitchen and turn to face the living room. Nettie isn't there, but the curtains are thrown open and moonlight paints the entire room in silver. The couch and the end tables are lit up and glittering. The front door is closed. Whatever I heard steal into the house isn't here. Not anymore.

I move to the window and lean my forehead against the glass. Out in the yard, two shapes come together and then apart. Vague outlines of two sisters, one whispering into the other's ear. Nettie. Carolina.

Nettie sees me first. Her mouth lifts into a smile, and she brings her fingers to her lips. Carolina sits behind Nettie, her knees dampened with dew and earth, and she braids Nettie's hair. Her fingers twitch like spiders through the strands, gardenias growing from her arms, her chest, and she places them in Nettie's hair, weaves her a night crown filled with white petals and sweet perfume.

They open their mouths, perfect round orbs that circle pearled teeth, but I cannot hear them, cannot hear the words they pass between them, and my heart aches with everything I've lost. I reach out to touch their skin, their hair, but there is only the cold glass under my fingers, and I pull my lips back from my teeth. I scream.

Nettie doesn't look at me again. Carolina never turns to face the window. Mama doesn't come out of her room. I am alone in this house, and the weight of it presses down, the scent of cherry blossoms thick in the air, and I think I'm drowning inside of it.

I lie down on the floor, close my eyes, and wait for the sound of footsteps against the porch, wait for the sound of the door opening, but it never comes. I count the space between my breaths and force my palms flat. I think again of Carolina, the July night when she first showed me the flowers, how we marveled at the thing she had become. But I had been afraid. Too afraid to follow her into the cold earth.

"I'm still afraid," I say, and I settle. I wait.

The entire world is coming undone. Everything shifting like gravel beneath my feet, and I flail, my hands beating against the thing shaking me.

"It's just me, Mack. It's okay. It's just me." Nettie kneels above me, her hair tangled and knotted with leaves and dead flowers.

The room seems to expand and then contract. In and out, I try to breathe but my lungs feel raw as if I spent the night gasping at frozen air.

"What did you do?"

Nettie presses her cheek to mine. Her skin is warm and flushed, and I catch the faintest trace of wisteria. I grab her wrist and wrench away so I can see her face.

"What did you do?"

She tugs at the collar of her shirt, pulls it away so I can see the faint purple impressions nesting against her skin.

"I thought it would hurt, but it didn't. Not even a little bit. And once it's there, blooming inside of you, everything lights up. Everything is so beautiful. We could all be together again. The way it's supposed to be," Nettie says, and I tuck my knees to my chest.

"Mama's dead you know. Swallowed a big bottle of pills. Not sure what they were, but Carolina told me."

"You're wrong."

"I'm not. When was the last time you heard her in there? Moving around or crying or anything at all?"

In the room down the hallway, Mama doesn't make a sound. I picture her on the bed, cocooned in blankets, her eyes still fixed on that point I'll never see. I don't want to go in there, not even to check and see if Nettie's right.

Nettie stands before me, her skin swirled and dotted with flora. Like a seed buried under the ground rupturing from spring earth. My sisters, blooming.

Carolina was able to keep the flowers hidden from everyone but Nettie and me. Wore long sleeves and pants and got dressed right after she took a shower. Even when she died, there was only that one violet I stole from her. All of the others bled away, were tucked somewhere safe inside of her so her body was smooth and unmarked. A deception wrapped in cold skin, and we kept her secret.

Nettie smooths her hands over the imprints of the petals and smiles. A secret smile. The smile Carolina carried on her lips for months before she drowned inside all of that sweetness.

"It's so much better this way," Nettie says and brushes my hair away from my forehead like Mama used to do when I was little and burning up with fever.

"You'll die."

She shrugs. "Not really."

"You won't be you anymore. You saw what Carolina is now."

"No. You're the one who didn't see."

I don't want to find her beautiful. Don't want to stare like someone bewitched as those pale blooms shift and change under her skin. I'm still afraid, but more than anything, I wish I didn't want them, too.

"Tonight," Nettie says and stands. Her feet are bare and streaked ink black with dirt. When she goes, she leaves the front door open, and December wind swirls through the room and catches at my hair.

I don't go to school the next day. Spend the morning and then the early afternoon in the hallway, my lips pressed against Mama's door, trying to work up the courage to call out for her or open the door or any goddamned thing other than standing there, but each time I do, my stomach clenches up, and I can't make myself do it.

I'm not sure where it is Nettie went. I searched the yard for her, shouted her name into the dark spaces hidden in the forest, but nothing answered me, so I went back into the house.

I go into our bedroom and lie down on Carolina's bed. "I should have opened the window," I whisper, and my skin burns. I want to be beautiful, too. I don't want to be the only one left behind.

Carolina never knew where the thing that changed her came from, if it was an angel or a demon or something else. She didn't have a reason for why all of those terrible, beautiful things found their way inside of her other than she was the one to open the window.

"Aren't you afraid?" I asked her the night it happened the first time.

"No. Of course not."

"What if it's something bad?"

"I don't care. How can anything so beautiful be bad?"

I was afraid for her. Fearful of the lovely things hiding under her skin, those feather light petals pushing through to make her something else. Something other. And I was angry for a while. Hid her favorite t-shirt and took her toothbrush and swiped it across the toilet seat. Angry because she'd been chosen instead of me, but then she started choking up blood.

I wait for the light to fail, for shadows to slip through the room, and I force myself up, force myself to move, to do anything other than lie there and wait for something to happen.

The front door is open again, and I pause at the threshold, look back at Mama's room, and then move out into the moonlight.

Carolina and Nettie stand in the middle of the yard, their hands clasped together, flowers erupting from their arms, their chests, their throats. Winding vines grown lush in the winter air and petals of sunshine, blush, violet, and cream twisting over and boring into bare skin.

"There's nothing left for us here, Mack," Nettie says, and petals fall from between her lips like the fairytale we used to read when we were girls.

"Nothing," Carolina says, and her voice is oil slick. The voice of something broken free from meat and bone. Full of light and sweet smells, my sisters smile and their eyes are luminous. Deep and dark as the night sky, and I feel myself leaning toward them.

"Stay here. With me," I say. I can't be sure if I'm speaking to Nettie or Carolina or both, and my throat knots.

Carolina comes to me first, her hands cool against my skin, and she presses her mouth to my face, drinks in my tears, and I collapse into her, let her fold me up tight, tight, tight, until I'm nothing. There is only her. This girl filled with flowers and darkness. My sister.

"We can't stay. Not like this. You know that."

"Please, Carolina."

Nettie kneels beside us. Her face is pale, drawn up as if whatever's inside of her is eating her up from the inside out. She vomits into the dust, the liquid a profusion of deep green, and her hands clutch at nothing.

"There's nothing left," Carolina says and extends her hand. Her skin ripples, the petals contained beneath thinly veiled, and I want to open my mouth, but everything stays frozen while Carolina holds me and Nettie retches in the dirt.

"For so long we've been second. Drifting and wondering when something would come along to take away everything that fell apart. A dead daddy and a Mama who looks at her three girls and sees only what she's lost. So much she lets them go," Carolina says, and Nettie lifts her head and wipes at lips gone crystalline.

"It's only us. Always us," Nettie says.

"And now?" I ask, but I don't want Carolina to answer. It's better to not think. To vanish inside the dream.

"And now," Carolina says and presses her lips to mine. "Say yes, sister. It will always be us. Growing strong."

Nettie puts her arms around me, and we sit there, together, crumpled against the ground like used up things that have been tossed away, and there is only us, only this unspoken need moving through me like water or fire, and I'm opening my mouth.

I'm opening my mouth, and Carolina breathes into me, honey sweet. Bees buzzing and warm spring air damp against my skin. Sisters bound together by flesh and petals. I open my eyes. Everything bright. Everything beautiful.

THE GHOST STORIES WE TELL AROUND PHOTON FIRES

Cassandra Khaw

Be careful with trusting navigation systems. Sometimes, they lie. They say there is a place where world ships go when they know the end is close. A prism of stars—ravenous, burning like abattoirs, striated by temporal anomalies and transcendentally sublime. If you go there, you'll see leviathanic corpses suspended between asteroids belts, their bones polished to incandescence by solar winds and cosmic debris. But don't get too close. Not every ship waits for its crew to evacuate first.

Still, if you make that mistake, all is not necessarily lost. If you're quick enough and clever enough, if you can inject the right code, the right algorithms before the first revenants appear—chances are you'll be fine. Ghosts, whether allegorical or discorporate victims of recursive timelines, only want space to sleep.

At least, that's what they say.

"You don't really believe there are spirits, do you?" drawls Fatimah through a mouthful of cherry-cola gum. The tips of her black hair are knife-frayed—stained cinnamon and lime.

Allen bristles. "There's no empirical evidence—"

"There's no empirical evidence that the sun isn't secretly rainbow-colored either," Fatimah retorts as she decants from her perch—an elegant motion, a gymnast's descent. She sweeps thick hair from a sharp-boned face, eyes liquid and bored. Against her brown skin, the vintage headphones, meticulously maintained, gleam like the ferryman's wages. "But you don't see anyone complaining about that."

He scowls. Fatimah grins. Were it not for the way she makes his pulse jackhammer against the membrane of his throat, the way her voice makes reason the exception, he wouldn't tolerate her. Allen's sure of that. *Stupid crush*, he thinks, before Fatimah's proximity devours all autonomy.

"You're sweating."

Stupid crush, he thinks again, a smile trembling on the cusp of being. "Yeah. Well. Might have something to do with the fact we're in the incinerator room."

Fatimah laughs and turns, the sway of her hips keeping time with the pounding of his heart, to strut up to the dormant trash compactor and pat it like a recalcitrant puppy. Allen tenses with the urge to follow, but he knows better to react before Fatimah commands, knows better than to volunteer a voice to the hungry silence.

"Since you believe in ghosts—"

"I never said—"

Fatimah laughs, a clear, silver music that cuts to his spine. "Since you believe in ghosts, I've got one for you. It's about the Nu Gui."

A pulse of recognition. "That's cheating. Teke-Teke is old world mythos."

"No." Fatimah disgorges a wad of chewed-up gum, and affixes it to the alloyed surface. It moans a whalesong reply and Allen twitches, like a man impaled on a jolt of electricity, eyes sliding away from the dark corners. If he just withholds acknowledgement, surely he can deny them existence, those jittering, electric tendrils in the margins of his eyesight. "She's not. Teke-Teke isn't just a construct of Old China. She's a metaphysical meme."

"This is lame, Fa—"

"They say—" a defiant interruption. Allen shivers, riveted. Fatimah's voice is silver, is gold resin, is entrapment honeyed and resonant, irresistible as the siren lure of a black hole. "— that myths can be divided into two categories: oral and memetic. One is deathless, one is not, surviving so long as the concept remains intact."

"That doesn't make sense." Allen purses his mouth. Neither adolescent lust nor fear of the known can counteract candor. "Oral tradition *is* memetic. That's the whole point. What you're saying is an oxymoron, and Fa—"

"You're making it too scientific."

"*I'm* making it too scientific?" Incredulity wells, hot, metallic. "You were the one teasing me about believing in ghosts and—"

"So you do believe in ghosts!"

"Argh!" Allen chucks his arms into the air, a hundred heartfelt profanities interlaced with that single expulsion of exasperation. "No! That's not what I meant! And even if I did, it's beside the point. *Anyway.* My point is you don't have a point."

His diatribe is received with a look and then discarded with a laugh. Fatimah tosses her hair and continues—relentless, triumphantly brazen.

"*They say*—" she begins again, stressing the words just so, with just enough charm to make Allen's heart jump. "—that the Nu Gui is the vengeful spirit of a suicide who meets their end in a bloom of red."

Allen feels eyes on the back of his hands, his mouth, his skin, and he shivers in reply to the weight of their scrutiny. "You mean they slit their wrists?"

"Ugh. You have no poetry—"

"This isn't exactly a laughing matter. You—"

"Whatever. Anyway, like I was saying, the Nu Gui is the spirit of a woman who either committed suicide while wearing red, or was buried in red. Ordinarily, it's a one in five billion chance that the dead will return, but something about that color pulls at them, especially those who died unfairly."

Here, Fatimah's eyes turn glassy, glazed, carefully pared of emotion, her mouth the dark slit of an emptied throat.

"So, what happens if you die while wearing a blue t-shirt?" Allen demands, eager to distract from whatever had hollowed her stare. Behind him, the room whispered, thickened, as though occupied by a thousand spectators. "You come back like an emo-goth?"

Fatimah shifts gears, swaps her solemnity for a vivid smile, the parabola of her mouth a star chart of secrets. "No clue. But I think it's time we find out if Nu Gui can be non-Chinese."

Before Allen can react, before he can devise a scream, a plea to desist, Fatimah presses a button, plunges an arm deep into the glowing maw.

Steel shrieks shut.

They say you should be careful when speaking to the neural matrices of your ancestors. Not all of them are real. They say that one in every twenty million is erroneous, a digital ego populated by serendipity; baseless, frameless, causal offspring of a thousand compromised archives.

The danger with these constructs is they are also parasitic—accidents in binary, input-starved and predatory. If you let them, they'll slither from network to neuron to nest quiet in the cup of your skull. There, they'll propagate, replicate, will complicate and instigate new branches of identity in the taxonomy of your memories, eliding fact into fabrication, until there is no "me" and only "we," a deep mind rife with maybes and never-could-bes.

There is no cure for that, they say. If they get you, you're as good as dead so watch out and read closely. Be careful, be slick. Be always vigilant against ghosts in grandparent skins.

"What do you think happens to the bodies?"

Allen glances at Fatimah. The uniform makes a stranger of her silhouette, more so than the fresh absence of her right arm, the limb ending smoothly beneath the elbow. It is constrictive, her attire, black synth-leather delineated in carbon fiber plating, oiled to a dull glow. Under the taut carapace, there is no gender, only power—coiled and subtle and anonymous.

"Which bodies?"

In the distance, three caskets drift among the cosmic debris. They were the last, had been the last on a ship pregnant with a million bright lives.

Don't think about that, Allen reminded himseslf. *Don't.*

"Those, obviously." She makes an irritated noise, gesturing with leather-gloved fingers. Her hair is too short, Allen catches himself thinking, surprised by the regret that epiphany triggers. "Earth had bacterium and vultures. Space has nothing."

"And?"

"It's a waste, isn't it? All that potential going to waste."

Waste. The word sang in his head.

"A veritable cornucopia of nutrients, carbon, and whatever else that life on Earth used to perpetuate itself," Fatimah continues—sad, savage. "All gone, left to wither like a compromised innocence."

Again, he feels it, that creeping wrongness, pimpling the curve of his spine. But Allen says nothing, only shrugs, hoping to elude his fears by way of ignorance. "The universe will survive."

"How long do you think it takes for our bodies to disintegrate out there?"

He sighs. The cadence of her thoughts is inscrutable, an entropic mess, so unlike the stern austerity of her garments, her station, closer to the girl she was than the woman she is. "Does it matter?"

"Doesn't it?"

A laugh shivers in Fatimah's ribs, mercury-cold and dangerous.

"I had a dream," she continues before Allen can stop her. "I had a dream that you were the ghost of a sea captain. Every night, you walked your vessel from end to end, looking out into the cold black ocean, always calling for someone."

Allen stills, breath lodged in his throat like a bullet. "Who?"

Fatimah laughs again, and this time the sound is wild, engine-roar, machine-death. "If this were most stories, this would be where I turn to you and say, 'Me.' But it's not.

You weren't calling for me. For a while, I thought it was you calling for justice, for me but not for me, if you know what I'm saying? Like you were the color red and I was a ghost who needed justice. But no. You weren't calling for those things either."

"What was I calling for then?"

"I can't tell you. The story isn't over yet."

They say that there was once a girl who was not real, a homunculus of photons and electro-impulses, illegal data-ghost, daemon; engineered by a young man's dream of a dead woman with a similar face, a similar name; kept functional by faith and fury and hope.

They were in love, were always meant to be in love; their attraction wasn't circumstantial, it was mandated by physics, irrevocable as the adagio of planets. But the universe is no place for love so potent, love so deep. Such beauty cannot exist without being balanced by tragedy.

And so, it sent death.

Some say it came asystolic-quiet. A cough, at first, wet and red. A discomfort in the ribs, an absence of hunger. Then, as a bloom of tumors, clotting in the gap between vertebrae. As convulsive fevers and dry-mouthed prayers, as a crescendo of anguish stuttering across hollow, sleepless months before at last, it all ended, and death crept from the room with her breath rattling in its lungs.

Some say it wasn't death who came courting, but the girl who sought quiet against the flat of a blade, who trussed herself up in claret and plunged into the void, who asked for respite against the clamor of an indifferent universe.

Whatever the case, all agree on this: she died and he did not. Some say he went mad from the loss, some say he only acquired the glacial clarity that comes on the other side of madness. In regards to this, there are a thousand truths, but none as lucid as the tensility of his attachment. He would not let go. No matter what was said to him, he would not tolerate the deletion of her existence, the slow disintegration of skeleton and skin. Before she could be interred in the cold of space, he ran, escaping with the pattern of her neurons, the chemical shape of her soul.

If death would take her from him, he would steal her back.

"What the fuck do you think you are doing? What the fuck? Turn the ship. Turn the fucking ship."

"I can't do this without you."

"All these people. You're going to kill the *entire fucking ship*."

"I can't! I can't—"

"*Allen, get out!*"

"I can't leave you."

"You're going to die! Turn around. Oh, God. We don't have time. We don't have time. We need to—you have to get out of here, you have to, you have to, *youhavetoyouhaveto—*"

They say he was a scientist, a captain, a liar with a honeyed tongue, a heartbroken trickster who brokered a hundred nations for the soul of his beloved. They say he killed himself, found respite at the end of the noose, the slant of a knife, that there was no redemption, only silence, the relief of an impartial dark.

They say he killed a ship of millions, that they screamed as they arrowed into the void, bodies decoalescing into protein and pain, bones dismantling into calcium extracts, stardust, and atoms of terrified memory.

They say he did nothing, that he lived on, that he found a new love and that love soon materialized into children, fair-haired and dark, a wealth of new joys to subsume the death of the old.

They say many things about him.

And if anyone asked, he would have told them they were wrong.

"I had a dream."

He startles at the hum of her voice—low, edged with the velvet roughness of sleep. Like a specter, Fatimah manifests beside him, silent, thoughtful, the heel of a palm pressed against a thick-lashed eye.

"Was it a dream about dying again?"

She yawns, stretches. In the halogen-limned penumbra, Fatimah is no more than thirteen, whole again, the lines of hard living scrubbed out, an image pilfered from their conjoined past, rebuilt into flesh and ragged cotton. "No. Not this time."

"What was it, then?"

"I dreamt about what came after."

Allen holds his breath. "And?"

"I died and then I woke up in a temporal anomaly, everywhere and nowhere at once, stretched between timelines. Our ship was dying. *I* was dying. But only dying. Death can't inhabit this environment, for this reason." She cups his cheek in a small hand, her thumb drawing circles across the three-day stubble.

He exhales into her palm, presses a kiss against the cool, callused skin. "No."

"It wasn't a dream, was it?"

"No." He says, heart roaring in his ears.

"Why, Allen? I remember *everything*. You could have—"

"I couldn't." The syllables fall in shivering clumps. Allen aches to hold her, to press lips to forehead, mouth to clavicle, to breathe in the scent of her hair, the warmth of her skin. But he does not.

"—had a proper life without me, outside of me."

"No. No, I couldn't."

"So, you'd rather have this? You'd rather be a ghost story?"

A filament of silence arches between them, glittering with a thousand things unsaid. Allen is riveted with the luminosity of her eyes, the nebula of emotions that spin in orbit around the axis of her pupils. He does not remember her ever being more beautiful.

"Yes."

She breathes in. Her eyes are bright and sad. "No."

"What do you mean 'no?'"

"What I mean is—" Fatimah slides long fingers over his own, pulls his hand down and flips his palm upright. Into the lines, she places a chaste kiss. "—you need to stop."

"I don't—"

"You can't stay here. I can't stay here. They can't stay here."

Allen hears them again, a susurrus of voices, more distinct than they've been in a thousand years. But he ignores them, the way they'd ignore him, when he begged at their door, pleading for a love already gone cold. It was always him and Fatimah. It would always be him and her.

"But—"

Now, Fatimah is eighteen, still thin as a wire, her cheekbones razor-straight, her hair a snarl of taut curls. She cups her hands over the back of Allen's head, eyes bruised, and pulls him close. "You have to let me go."

"I told you," he says again, this time with more vehemence, less force. "I can't."

But she does not listen. *She never does*, Allen thinks, furious, before her lips find his and there is suddenly nothing else but the memories clotting in his throat like tears. "Once upon a time, there was a boy."

Her voice is clear and silver and sweet as despair, and it is all he can do to not weep.

"And he loved a girl very much. But the girl died. He would not have it, though, and so, he chased her into the dark. Unfortunately, he forgot something important. He forgot to leave himself a trail. In his haste to find her, he became trapped."

Allen dampens his mouth. "Maybe, it was intentional."

A smile flickers. "Death *happens*, Allen. We're destined to die. Some of us earlier than others, sure. Some of us by accident, some of us by choice, but it happens. And you can't just...stay *here*."

"I can," Allen retorts, hating the petulance coarsening his rebuttal, the way it sharpens each syllable into a resentful whine. "And I have."

"You can't. You can't just stay here." Fatimah withdraws, thirty-nine now and dressed in military attire.

He blinks.

Now, she is twenty-six, buxom from motherhood, the nurse she became in a parallel existence.

Another blink.

Eight. Seventy. Fifty-two. Even as Allen watches, her form continues to coruscate between every variant of her. Only the smile remains constant, too heavy with grief to participate in the temporal fluctuations.

"I won't let you."

"What?"

Too late, he registers the seismic hymn of the propulsion

engines, the adjustment of ballast and gears, an ecosystem of preparations, too many to name. Too late, he realizes her intentions, even as Fatimah takes another step back.

"Let go. I've done so a million years ago."

"No." It is not a shout, not even a word spoken, just a gasp of noise, a stolen breath.

The world turns white.

"I love you."

And suddenly, he is elsewhere.

GARNIER

Brian Evenson

I. Not Garnier

I sold the house simply because my wife and I had been planning to sell it. I understand it might seem strange to some, particularly in the light of her sudden disappearance, but try to understand the matter from my perspective. From *our* perspective, I should say. It was simply a question of me proceeding as we, as a couple, had intended to proceed. I was, in this as in all things, following my wife's wishes.

Even so, I hesitated longer than I suspect my wife would have desired, just in case she might reappear. A week, then another, then a third. I would have waited even longer had not Garnier informed me that though he was still game to purchase the house, he would not be so for much longer.

So, you see, it is simple: Garnier is to blame for my selling the house. It was Garnier who forced my hand.

You might say that my wife brought Garnier into our lives, but it would be more accurate to say that she brought Garnier into *my* life. She had known him before, apparently for years. How she first met him was never quite clear to me, and her elucidation of the matter was, at best, elusive. *Did you have a romantic relationship?* I asked her once, unclear as to what exactly their connection had been. Of course not, she claimed, laughing nervously, how could I think such a thing? They had been friends, just friends. And yet when I asked Garnier the same question, he offered a quite different response.

"Brother," he said, clapping one hand upon my shoulder. "What's past is in the past."

"Pardon?" I said.

"Exactly," he said. "Pardon. We must pardon."

"But who exactly do I need to pardon?" I asked him, "and for what?" But he had already turned away.

I don't mean to suggest that Garnier had anything to do with my wife's disappearance. When I somewhat indignantly informed my wife of this conversation, she simply laughed. "Darling," she said, "you know how Garnier is. He didn't mean anything." After a little more coaxing, some verbal, some sexual, I was inclined to agree with her.

No, Garnier had nothing to do with it. If I had any suspicion whatsoever, why would I have sold Garnier our house?

We made, as we say here, a private arrangement. I listed the house at a certain price and Garnier officially purchased it for that, though he also would secretly give me an additional amount in cash. This is how it is done here—it is a way of avoiding excessive taxes. Even the tax collectors know it is done and they do it too when they purchase a house. Garnier and I went to the recording office and signed the papers and shook hands, and then, after, made our way back to the house, the house which had been mine and now was his.

We sat at the table. My things, my wife's things, were still in the house. Boxes were scattered throughout the rooms. I planned to have them and the furniture removed the next day and placed in storage. I took the extra keys from the sideboard and placed them on the table, then slid them clinking toward him.

He stared down at the keys, but did not pick them up.

"Shall we have a drink?" he asked. "The two of us? The remainder?"

I nodded my assent. It was only after a moment of both of us sitting there in silence, staring at one another, that I realized he expected me to be the one to stand and fetch the bottle, despite it no longer being my house.

I stood and made my careful way to the cabinet. It was empty; of course, it had been packed. I bent and broke the tape sealing a box on the floor below it. I grasped the neck of a bottle of table wine and then thought twice and brought out instead the whisky and two thick-glassed tumblers. I turned. He sat there at the table, his back to me, his body perfectly balanced, poised. Garnier had always been like that, not a wrinkle, not a hair out of place. For a moment I had an almost overwhelming desire to break the bottle over his head and watch him slide, head bloody, from his chair.

I closed my eyes.

When I opened them again, Garnier was still alive, still unharmed, still just as poised. I made my way to my chair as if nothing had happened, which was, in fact, the case.

We clinked glasses. He took a drink, a long one. I sipped at mine.

"What a dirty business," Garnier said, and for a moment I wasn't sure what he was speaking about. And then he added, "Where do you suppose she's gone?"

I shrugged. "How should I know?"

He was, I realized, staring at me, intensely. I stared back, my expression bland, unblinking, as if I were a mannequin.

"About our private arrangement," I said, and trailed off.

A flicker of irritation passed over his face. He looked down at the tumbler he was rolling around in his palm.

"You know," he said to the tumbler, "perhaps I am not so inclined to honor our private arrangement. The papers have been signed. The deal is done. Who cares what was agreed to privately once the public agreement is completed?"

I didn't say anything. He looked up sharply. "What do you say to that?" he said. "Why do you not say 'Do not cheat me, Garnier?' Do you really allow me to speak to you in such fashion?"

"These words do not mean anything, Garnier," I said slowly. "I know you are an honorable man."

Did I truly believe this? No, I did not. Whatever else Garnier was, he was hardly honorable. But what mattered was that Garnier himself thought so. I swallowed. My mouth, I found, was surprisingly dry.

"You are an honorable man," I said evenly, "and for this reason you will pay not only what we agreed, but more."

For a long time he stared at me, astonished, and then slowly his mouth widened into a grin. A moment later, his valise was on the table, the notes being carefully counted out in neat stacks before me. And then he had stood to remove his wallet from his pocket, making a final thin stack of all the notes pressed within. He bent down and kissed the top of my head.

"There," he said. "I have discharged my obligation. What I owe plus thirty pieces of silver. I am no longer in your debt. Do you agree?"

I nodded.

"You are now my tenant," he said, "and I am your landlord."

"Just until tomorrow," I said.

But he seemed to be paying no attention. He had already moved across the room and out into the salon. I stayed at the table, motionless. A moment later, I heard the front door open and close. Garnier was gone.

Why, I wondered after he was gone, had he given me more than he had promised? Why had he smiled? Knowing Garnier, knowing what I knew about Garnier, it made no sense. No, Garnier was the sort of man to discharge his obligations to the penny but, like all rich men, pay not a penny more. Or so I had believed. Either Garnier was not the man I had thought him to be, or he felt himself, for reasons that I did not understand, to be more in my debt than I had realized.

I stood and placed the bottle in the cabinet. I would leave it and the two tumblers for Garnier, as a momento. I carried the tumblers to the sink and ran tepid water into them. I had just turned them over, and placed them on the floor of the sink to dry, when the doorbell rang.

I dried my hands and made my way to the door, expecting to see Garnier, come perhaps to accuse me, to say all he had not managed to say since my wife's disappearance.

But it was not Garnier at the door. It was a policeman, two specialists in forensic gear stationed behind him.

"Yes?" I said. "Can I help you?"

"We're here to search the house," he said.

"Search the house?" I repeated. "Who gave you permission?"

"The owner," he said.

"But I am the owner," I said, and then stopped. Of course, I was no longer the owner.

"Are you," said the policeman, glancing down at a piece of paper in his hand, "Mr. Garnier?"

For a moment I hesitated, then I smiled. "In a manner of speaking," I said. I opened the door and bowed. "Gentlemen," I said, "please come in."

II. Garnier

You must understand it from my perspective. I had lost Julianne, perhaps due to my own foibles, my lack of appreciation for what I had in her, and then I had, completely by accident, found her again. One moment I was, as usual, simply stopping to fill my car with gas just off the autoroute, and the next there she was, coming out of the convenience store, a packet of crisps in her hand. Or perhaps not crisps—a sweet perhaps or something less romantic, a newspaper. How am I meant to remember? I was not looking at what was in her hands—I was looking at her, my own hands beginning to shake, as I thought, *Am I dreaming?*

For surely I was dreaming. She looked as young as she ever had, though it had been a decade. *You have finally cracked, Garnier,* I told myself. *From now on, you will remake the world into a world you would prefer, one with Julianne in it again. She will walk past you again and again, everywhere you go, as fugitive and fleeting as a ghost.*

But then she stopped, staring at me. "Garnier?" she said. And then, with a smile, "Garnier!"

Did I embrace her? Yes, of course I embraced her. Why would I not? She was my Julianne.

"Julianne," I said, "about what happened, please, allow me to explain."

Only then did I see a flicker of fear in her eyes. "No, no," she said. "Let me explain." She carefully broke away from me and tugged me around. There, standing behind me, was a man, diminutive in stature, ugly in face, with a child's hands—more a model not-to-scale for a man rather than a man proper. A gas station attendant, I presumed. "Garnier," she said, "let me introduce you to my husband."

From surprise, I gave a barking laugh. It was a joke, surely. But when I realized that, no, she was serious, I did as any gentleman would do and moved forward, grinning desperately, to crush his hand in my own.

I deliberately did not ask her where they lived. A plan, you see, was already forming in my head. I traced them by their license plate. It was a small matter to uproot myself to her town. A smaller matter still to feign surprise when I first saw her on the street of said town, and to explain why a redistricting of territories at my place of employment had shifted my territory and necessitated my move. How was I to know this was her town? What a remarkable coincidence. Surely, it must mean something...

The husband was less easily convinced. He was, as they say, the suspicious type—though perhaps in this case correct to be so. "How were the districts redrawn?" he began by asking, as if from simple curiosity, and then, "But didn't you have the seniority to choose which territory would be yours?" Before I knew it, I was doing verbal acrobatics to avoid putting my foot in my mouth.

I knew from the moment I first saw her again that Julianne and I would have a lengthy affair. Why would I have moved to her town otherwise? What I did not know was how passionate it would become. She was, I came to feel, the love of my life, and I was the love of hers. *My husband must not know,* she said, when it was clear that what we had was no passing fling. *Why?* I said. *Shouldn't we tell him so that we can be together?* She shook her head. *He is dangerous,* she said. *We must plan carefully, and then, before he suspects, we must leave, and leave no trail behind.*

I must admit I laughed. That half-man, that homunculus of a husband, dangerous? How could it be possible? But I am not laughing now.

No, I am not laughing now. I am thinking, rather, that he must have found out and done something to Julianne. If we are lucky, she and I, she is chained in a dark hole somewhere. If we are not lucky, she is still in a dark hole, but it is a dark hole filled with dirt.

Have I told the police that she and I were having an affair? No, I have not. If I tell them as much, they will assume that I am to be suspected. But I am not to be suspected—he is. And there are a few things I have found in my house since her disappearance that lead me to think that the husband intends for the police to throw their suspicious onto me. A pair of her underthings underneath the armoire—which I suppose it is possible to explain as something she left behind after one our trysts, but I know she did not. And when I found these, I made a thorough search, even going so far as to discover, secreted in the crawlspace beneath the house, one of her shoes, its toe spattered brown with dried, degraded blood. Was it really her shoe? I did not know, not for certain, but I think so. Who else's could it be? Did a shoe come there, under the house, by accident? No, of course not: it was placed there and is meant to be found, but not by me: by the police.

But I have not made myself a suspect, for I have told the police nothing of our affair. I have not played the role of the indignant lover casting aspersions on the husband. And the husband, not knowing what to do to entrap me, simply waits, like a spider. I have installed cameras around my property, trying to catch him leaving something else, something of hers, as a means to entrap me, but he has grown savvy. He waits.

And so, we are at an impasse. I watch his house, waiting for him to reveal something. He reveals nothing. I return home to examine the footage from my cameras, even though I know I will not see a single image of him. He is too careful for that. It terrifies me that he will be willing to be satisfied with punishing his wife if he cannot safely punish me.

And me? What will I be satisfied with? Can anything satisfy me?

I offered to buy the husband's house, thinking that if I do I might find something in it, some trace of her, some sense of where he has taken her. It is unlikely, but it is not impossible. He was, surprisingly enough, enthusiastic—he claimed that he and Julianne had long wanted to sell, that it was "what she would want." Very good, I said. *After all,* he continued, *the two of you were so close,* and then he named an exorbitant price. I accepted. He balked, claimed that perhaps he should wait, a day or two, a week or two, just in case she returned. I nodded my acknowledgment and then did my best to observe him and his house, to try to ensure that he could not destroy any evidence of his wife's demise. If I saw him scrubbing a floor, or burning articles of clothing, or doing anything else that might be deemed suspicious, I told myself, I would rush in and restrain him and then call the police.

And yet, he did nothing suspicious. He came home. He read a book. He went to bed. Night after night it was always the same, and no matter how long I stayed shivering in the darkness, nothing changed.

In the end, I became impatient. I told him I must have the house now or not at all. Still, I was surprised when he agreed to sell it to me.

As soon as he had, as soon as I was officially the owner, before he had even moved out of the house, I called the police. I told them I had had an anonymous telephone call indicating that the fellow whose house I had just bought had murdered his wife. Was it true they had no suspects? Could they not, I begged, search the property for her remains? I, as the new owner of the house, gave them my blessing to do so.

They found nothing. No spattered blood, no residue, nothing moved, nothing out of place. *Perhaps*, I thought for a fugitive moment, *she really has run off*. But no, I was sure, he had killed her.

But if not in his own house, where?

I am leaving these notes where they will not be found without a careful search. I have tucked them deep in the crawlspace under the house, where I previously found the shoe. I am going to confront the husband. Perhaps he will reveal something. Or perhaps I will simply return here, in an hour, two, having learned nothing, and to simply record that fact.

III. Not Garnier

It is true, I killed him, I will not deny it, but I did so strictly in self-defense. He came here, you see, to kill me.

I was, as I had done every evening, sitting here, reading, praying that I would suddenly hear my new wife open the door and readmit herself into my life as if nothing had happened. Her disappearance had been a shock, and so sudden that I could not but believe it would come to an end just as suddenly.

When there came a knock at the door, I thought at first it must be her. My heart leaped, from joy, from fear. *But why?* I considered, just before my fingers brushed the knob, *Would she knock? No, she would just come in.* And so I was not surprised to open the door and find not her, but Garnier.

"Hello, Garnier," I said.

"May I come in?" he asked, the muscles in his jaw tightening as if he were deliberately attempting to deform one side of his face.

"Of course," I said smoothly, and admitted him. "I must apologize," I said. "I expected to be out by now, but the police left things in a certain disarray. It will take me a day or two longer than expected."

Garnier choose not to answer.

"Won't you sit down?" I asked. "Won't you have a drink?"

He took a breath.

"You killed her," he said.

"Who?" I couldn't stop myself from saying, and then immediately added, "You're mad."

"Mad?" he said. "I don't think so. What about the shoe under my house?"

"A shoe under your house?" I said. "What does that have to do with me? It's your house."

"And so is this," he said.

We spoke further. What we said is hardly important and, in any case, I can hardly remember it. I was too busy paying attention to the erratic nature of his gestures, wondering if and when he would attack me. He is a large man, much larger than me, and I have to admit I was quite frightened. All the time he spoke, I was positioning myself, moving closer to the counter in the kitchen, trying to do so without him noticing, looking for something to protect myself with. Which is why, when he did attack, I had the butcher knife close at hand.

I did not stab him. I merely brandished the blade as a defense. He charged at me and fell on the knife. The autopsy should make that clear. Or if I did stab him, if the autopsy shows that, it was only by reflex, to defend myself.

In any case, Garnier is dead and I am sorry for it. And yet, I am still confused: why would he accuse me of murdering my wife? To be honest, in accusing me he seemed as if he were trying to convince himself. Could he truly believe it? Surely not. I loved my wife. I loved her deeply. So much so that even when she told me she was having an affair with Garnier I forgave her. We embraced one another, we cried. She would, she told me, break it off with Garnier, would let him know immediately. Except that, suddenly, she was gone.

Why did I not tell you this before? I had no proof against Garnier. I was honestly convinced that my wife, wherever she was, would eventually make her way back on her own. What need was there to malign Garnier until I knew for certain?

But now he is dead, and there is no maligning the dead. I still do not believe him—I cannot: this talk of a shoe under the house is the gibbering of a madman, an ex-lover driven mad by grief.

No, if you look under the house, I am sure you will find nothing there, nothing at all.

But still, you should check. If only to clear Garnier's name. Yes, check, for that reason alone. The poor madman.

And when you have looked, let me know what, if anything, you find. I will be here, waiting.

LOVE STORY, AN EXORCISM

Michelle E. Goldsmith

Your clubhouse is a cleared space beneath the wattles—three walls of foliage, and the fourth the outer side of someone's back fence, a floor of dry grey dirt where you've meticulously swept all the leaf litter away. Through the gaps between branches, an assortment of rusty play equipment is visible, complete with the requisite unimaginative graffiti—Terry eats Dicks, Marks a gay fag, CUNT!!!—and a forest of oddly proportioned phalluses on the side of the slide.

You search for patterns in this scrawl as though it's some kind of alien code, some puzzle that, if solved, might yield the answer to end your torment. Desperate, you grasp for something, anything that might appease Amy—your best friend, your interrogator.

Tightening her grip on your arms, she leans in to press her face close to yours. You turn your head to the side. Her breath is hot on your cheek.

Holding dead still, you let the earsplitting song of the cicadas in the trees above reverberate through your skull, begin to transport you.

Amy's fingernails dig deeper into the soft flesh of your wrist. You try not to react.

Someone's bound to come past soon. Some bushwalkers probably, heading home as the sun lowers in the sky, coming back up the path from the nearby state forest where, last summer, you discovered a wattle tree hanging with hundreds of bulbous, orange cocoons, like ugly Christmas decorations made from hardened Cheetos.

You picture them rounding the corner—imagine the crunch of their boots on the twigs and gravel. Maybe if you try hard enough you can will them into being.

"Tell me!" Amy spits, shaking you. "Tell me what they say about me when I'm not there!" It's the same demand she's been repeating for what feels like hours. She's got you backed up against the fence, arms restrained, splinters pricking your shoulder blades through the cotton of your t-shirt. The clasp of your watch digs into your skin where it presses against the wood. You want to squirm, but don't dare.

"I know they talk about me. I know it! There's something you're not telling me out of loyalty to Jess."

There isn't. Although you consider making something up. But you can't work out what response she wants.

What satisfies Amy and what only enrages her more is ever unpredictable, the right answer an erratically moving target. She twists her grip on your arm until you're sure the skin will split. Your heart rate elevates. Your guts churn with anxiety like imminent diarrhea.

But someone *has* to come down the path soon. It must be getting late. And even if they don't, she'll have to let you go eventually. You glance down at your watch. The bright digital display counts down the last few minutes to 6 p.m., the hour by which you swore you'd be home. Sky blue, chunky and conspicuously new, the watch was a gift from Jess, your second-best friend, for your tenth birthday three days ago.

Amy inhales loudly. Did she see you look at the watch? She's silent for a moment and when she speaks again her voice is lower, softer, more sincere.

"Jess says things about you, you know. Gross things. That's how I know she must talk about me. She says that your parents are related. That you're an incest baby. That's why your dad left."

It's an unconvincing lie. The words sound far too much like Amy's.

"You shouldn't protect someone who says that," she says. "I told you what she said about you. Now I need to know what she says about *me*."

If it could, her glare would burn you, peel away your skin in curling strips.

You can't think of anything to say. Can't seem to think past a mad dash up the hill towards home, even though Amy, much taller, much faster, despite your similarity in age, would surely catch you before you got half way.

A strangled growl erupts from Amy's throat and she shoves you sideways. Your elbows scrape against the fence on your way to the ground.

She's on you before you can clamber up, grappling with you in the dirt, tearing the watch from your arm. When she has it, she runs full bolt towards the playground. At the retaining wall she stops and throws the watch down on a big, oil-stained boulder. Then, she grabs a smaller rock from its place in the wall and pounds it down onto the watch, over and over, until the gift is in pieces. As you look on, she brushes the parts to the ground and steps on them, grinding with her heel.

Later, when you arrive home, unforgivably late, your mother wants to know where your new watch is, why your clothes are filthy and your elbows grazed. You tell her you and Amy were playing hide and seek in the bushland and you must have lost the watch somewhere in the scrub. So careless. For the rest of the evening the few words she addresses to you have a razor edge. But you can deal with that. You go to bed relieved. The worst was over as soon as you got home. With the lights out you reach down to pat your German Shepard, Kally, where she lies on her mat beside your bed, and whisper the whole story to her.

A year later you and Amy are sitting across from each other in the crowded shopping centre food court, scoffing McDonalds while you wait for her mum to return from buying cake-decorating supplies. You look up from taking a sip of Coke to find Amy staring into your face, an odd twist to the line of her mouth. She erupts into laughter.

"You're ugly." She struggles for breath between hysterical bursts. "You're so fucking ugly!"

You look to the people at adjacent tables, sure that everyone must be staring at you. But they continue picking at their greasy meals, talking among themselves, joining lines for fast food. They're like extras in a bad soap, overly conscious of their role not to draw attention to themselves. Passive, unreactive, they fade into the backdrop. Perhaps, if you asked, one of them could teach you that trick.

Amy laughs so hard she cries, doubled over with her nose touching her squashed cheeseburger.

Here's a question for you.
How many times can you break a wrist falling off monkey bars?

What if you hate monkey bars—the metal smell they leave on your hands reminding you too much of blood—and you haven't played on them for years?

How many times then?

When you're both twelve, Amy wants to know why you never stay over at her house, why she always has to come to yours. She won't let the question drop, asks it at least a dozen times every time you meet.

You make up excuses. You can't tell her the truth. That her family creeps you out, that you hate traversing the random junk that covers every surface of their two-story house. You can't admit that you get tired of listening to her talk about the other girls in your class, her constant harping on about how they're "bad influences."

Did you know that Jess wants to fuck your Sixth Grade teacher? That her mum already did? Actually, they both did. On your desk while the class budgie watched.

Amy's stories don't always make sense.

You know she gets jealous. She doesn't like it when you speak to other girls. Why would you want other friends when nobody will ever love you like she does?

You can never let her find out you're avoiding her. That sometimes she's too intense and it scares you. That some days you'd rather stay home with your dog and the curtains drawn, ignoring the doorbell when it rings.

Amy grows frustrated with you more and more frequently. You can't seem to go a day without arguing, without her accusing you of something.

Whenever she doesn't know what you've been doing she

suspects you've been hanging out with someone else, making new friends and loving them better. Seeing as you've just started at different high schools, this means she's suspicious most of the time.

You've betrayed her. You're false. How could you do this? You're such a liar.

Not that it matters. Not that she *cares*.

She has plenty of other friends, she assures you. All prettier and funnier and just plain *better* than you. The names she gives them change every week.

It doesn't matter that her suspicions are baseless. That you haven't betrayed her. You're too shy, too nervous around strangers to make new friends easily. Nothing you say can convince her.

Sometimes she hits you, suddenly and for no reason at all. Then she stops and acts as though it never happened despite the red marks that still sting your flesh.

Sometimes you think about the last time you stayed over at her house—the night her younger brother tried to smother you with a pillow in your sleep. You wonder whether the only reason she stopped him was because she wanted to be the one to kill you herself.

You are twelve and a half, and good at school, but the answer to this question evades you.

As the months pass, Amy becomes more and more obsessed with sex. She brings it up in almost every conversation.

She knows things now, she tells you. Knows *all* about them. She's heard older kids talking in the toilet blocks. Her parents let her stay up late watching R-rated movies on cable. You don't even have cable, so you'll have to take her word for it.

She tells you that every man you know will rape you if given the chance. So will some of the women. "That's just how they are," she says. It's all you're good for.

She tells you a lot of things. That you're a *frigit*, though you only have a vague idea what that means. That nobody will ever love you. That nobody ever could except for her.

Amy says that lezzos burn in the devil's pit. She's quite certain about this one.

But then why, every night that she stays over, must you fear her hands creeping over to find you in the dark?

At thirteen, you need to start hiding the hand-shaped bruises on the insides of your thighs.

It's summer, and you and Amy are in your backyard, throwing a grotty tennis ball for Kally and swatting away the evening's first mosquitos.

Amy bounces the ball hard against the side of the house, sending it ricocheting across the lawn, and Kally bounds off to retrieve it. As you stand there beside her waiting for your turn to throw, Amy hits you. She strikes you hard across the face and you stumble back, surprised.

Before you can react, your dog has her by the leg, is tearing into her, ripping skin and flesh from her calf in a rapid, shaking motion. You've never seen so much blood. Amy screams, and then you scream. Kally releases her, looking confused, and then trots up to sniff at your shoe as you stand there, staring, for a few long moments before you run for the phone. Your mum rushes Amy to the emergency room, paying for her stitches and the tetanus shot.

"What happened?" your mum asks. "Did anything trigger Kally to attack? Was she acting strange beforehand?"

"No," Amy says, wiping tears from her cheeks. "It came out of nowhere."

You nod agreement, unaware of what you're really being asked.

Your mum talks to Amy's. It isn't really that surprising, the adults agree. The dog is almost fourteen, half-blind, losing it a little. These things can happen as animals age. It's sad, but that's the way things are. We should have seen it coming.

Amy's parents want Kally put down.

You don't actually believe it will happen. Surely something will stop it, someone will intervene. But then it's already done.

Afterwards, your mum returns home from the vet lugging a big black garbage bag. The plastic clings in places, doing little to disguise its contents. Mum heads out the back and soon you hear the scrape of a spade slicing earth.

You long to run out and snatch the bag, to rip it open and hug Kally's body to your own, to never let go, to just stay there until the flesh and fur falls away from her bones and you slowly starve to death, until all that's left are two skeletons locked together—more than you deserve. But you can't move. All the breath seems to have been sucked out of your lungs.

"It's kinder this way," your mum tells you later that night as you sob into your blankets. "She was old and had arthritis and didn't know what she was doing anymore. She couldn't be trusted around children. She would've just become more unpredictable. She loved you though, as much as a dog can, and that's what matters."

At fourteen, you add the death of your true best friend to the growing list of things for which you cannot forgive yourself.

You and Amy begin to drift apart. She visits less and less frequently.

But when you do see her, she tells you that she sees demons. They are all over your house, haunting seemingly innocuous objects—toys, books, a hand-painted wooden egg your aunt brought back from Samoa.

The first time she says this you laugh, thinking you're going to tell each other ghost stories, lock yourselves in your mum's walk-in wardrobe with a torch like old times. Then you realize she's serious.

"It's not funny," she says.

These demons will possess you. Possibly they already have. Don't you understand that she's risking her soul just to be here talking to you?

You start trying to hide any potentially incriminating belongings before she comes over, racing around the house shoving anything you think she might decide is sacrilegious into closets and under beds. But she always finds something.

Finally it happens, the thing you always feared. The thing you always knew would happen anyway. Amy decides that you can no longer be her friend. She says your presence is tainting her, ruining her. You cry. But they are tears of pain and relief intermingled.

For years afterwards, you get a feeling like insect legs prickling under your skin whenever you pass Amy's house on your way to the school bus stop. You remember clearly the house's layout, the path from the front door to Amy's room. But eventually, even high school ends. You move away for uni. Reminders of Amy become fewer and less frequent.

Occasionally you still think about her. You wonder where she is and what she's doing now. You heard she joined a cult. That she's dead. That she has a baby now and another on the way.

You try to guess at what made her the way she was. Abuse? Neglect? Lack of discipline? Genetics? Or was it true what she said on that last day you saw her? Could it be that your presence was sullying her is some way? Causing her moral decay? Inciting her to depravity?

Perhaps some people should never be close to one another, should be kept apart like violently reactive chemicals. Or like a lycanthrope and the light of a full moon.

Were you some kind of catalyst for a dangerous transformation?

Was it your fault?

You'll never be sure. You'll have to live with this uncertainty.

Over time other questions begin to nag at you. If you ran into Amy some place now, how would you react? Would you both pretend you were strangers and none of it ever happened? Or would the same reaction occur again?

And if it did, would things play out the same? Who now would be the stronger? Who would be the least broken by the years that separate you, the most hardened, the best equipped to hurt the other? Could it be you who is the wolf disguised, hungry for flesh, and she who is the moon? An anticipatory tingle runs through your limbs.

At twenty-eight, you return to your family home, having agreed to housesit while your mum spends six weeks in Europe.

It's a humid summer evening, electrified with the cries of cicadas. Sitting on the back verandah, you look out across the unchanged yellowed lawn, where once you played and had water fights and threw the ball for Kally. You linger on the spot beneath the lemon tree where once rose a mound of earth, which settled, month by month, until you had only memory to remind you what was buried there.

You itch with a creeping restlessness. You need to stretch your legs before it gets too dark. There were walking tracks nearby, weren't there? You don't set out with a particular destination in mind, but by the time you reach the end of your street it's clear where you're going.

There's still a playground, although it's not the one you remember. The old graffiti-covered slide, the familiar rust-flaky monkey bars—they must've been torn down sometime in the intervening years. Now, in their place, stands colorful, blocky new play equipment, all matching and safety standard certified and plastic. You ignore the urge to sit on the swing. Something else calls to you, beneath the song of the insects, tugging at the threads of your memory, urging you on.

Your gaze alights on a familiar copse of wattles at the park's edge.

The trees have grown and the foliage is denser, but you manage to push through the branches, collecting only a few scrapes and scratches before emerging into the space between the trees and the fence.

You kneel down and, with bare hands, sweep away the leaf litter to reveal the dusty soil beneath.

The drone of cicadas intensifies. The sound envelops you, seems to become a part of you, filling your skull and chasing all painful, buzzing, tormenting thought out through your ears.

You begin to dig.

Slowly at first, scooping handfuls of dirt from the clubhouse floor and into a mound against one wattle trunk. But the deeper you go the more urgent your motions become. Soon you're breaking through roots and ripping out dirt clods with your nails, tearing at the earth in a frenzy, heedless of the pain some part of you still knows you should feel. Deeper down, the dirt is darker, richer and cooler. You breathe deeply of its organic scent and continue digging.

At last, you stop. For a few moments, you are frozen in a meditative stillness as your heart rate stabilizes. Then you reach down into the hole.

You kneel there, before the shallow grave you've unearthed, its collection of old bones, fractured in odd places, now scattered all around you. In your palm are fragments of what might once have been a digital watch with a blue plastic band.

You kneel there, motionless beneath the wattles as blood drips from your torn fingernails, as the shadows deepen and dusk falls, as the cicadas continue to sing.

AN ENDING (ASCENT)

Michael Wehunt

Our graves will be a museum. A place where people come seeking a sense of what it was like to die, trailing through the rows of headstones until they find the youngest, the last of us. It could be they'll stop at mine. I picture them standing there: It's not quite raining, there's a mist that settles on their coats in the moment of silence they give to me but mostly to themselves. Relief like a cold, pure breath released into the sky, if they've managed to keep the atmosphere clean. There are moments, plenty of them, I find myself hoping they haven't.

The story of my life will be etched into the marble, slowly dimming in the seasons. I don't know what the second date will tell them. I only know the first, and it is the reason they will come.

—*November 25, 1979*

They'll count the days between my birth and the Age

Line. Thirty-eight. The weight of their voices, raw and respectful and relentless, saying, *He was so close.* They'll observe the old rites, while the novelty holds, stoop to lean irises or lilies beneath the month, beneath the year. And they'll straighten and pull each other closer, as though against the damp. Looking out over all those monuments.

It's almost a comfort, this thought. I try to make it one. But only the slow rusting quiet will come when they no longer do, though we who remain cannot know the quality, the tone of that quiet, when the earth is left behind like a husk.

My mind circles back and back to these things, these pictures. They leave me dull as a moth kept from light. Because I so recently fled from a graveyard, yes, and because I've returned to stand in the hallway of my home and listen to my wife and the lover she's taken, their whispered grunts, the rhythm of the headboard tapping the wall. I open the bedroom door and the first thing I see before I close my eyes is the window looking out on the old cottonwood, the white sky cut into confetti through its branches.

A gasp, a scrambling within the sheets that pool around their slickened forever bodies. "Caithlin." I say it again, louder but still numbed and too far from a shout. She's not even hiding it anymore, not in any concerted way. There are all the conversations we haven't had about the friendship she's rekindled with Terrence Dutil. Her late nights at the university, his visits to the house to help in her garden out back. How she carries her tether book from room to room, and in bed tilts the pale blue wash of its light away from me. All the clues arranged like careless furniture, and now that I'm standing here, forgetting to breathe, I admit to myself why I've been stepping around them.

"John, honey, I'm sorry, you weren't supposed to be home until tomorrow." Her words in a single blurred rush, running hot and cold at once. I keep my eyes clenched shut like a child's.

Terry murmurs his own stream of words but my mind is wet enough with resignation and I can't bear to listen. I rewind myself, step back into the hall, and let a throb of quiet cover the sound of Caithlin telling him to get dressed. I stand in the family room staring half-lost into the video wall's screensaver, which is looping panoramic stills of our grandson splashing through Pacific foam, and I say, slowly, feeling every tick and tap of my tongue against my teeth, "I am the only one who is going to die."

This anger, always at a slow burn. Knowing it is a selfish thing only dampens it so much. I flushed the antidepressants two weeks ago. Close to a hundred blue, government-sanctioned capsules. They had turned me into glass, a window I could only look through, and did little more than wrap the ache and hide it like a telltale heart.

Dr. Hinton recommended I connect with my parents, try to accept that I am of their era. Embrace my past, since it is no less primitive than my future. The good doctor has suggested many things since I was ushered out of my job at the accounting firm, most of them steeped in time. He preaches technology dissociation, foremost the surrender of my tether, all the networks and bells and whistles. Go into nature, go into where you came from, John. It's the only thing you can take with you.

But a few hours in Vermont and I found I could no longer abide the close green country folding around me. The cemetery outside Montpelier was held in a bowl of mountains, the grass too eager around my parents' graves and their parents' graves behind them. Their tiny beloved church a postscript there in the wilderness. I felt cloistered by the hunched forests, the Appalachian peaks mossy teeth jutting above them, the air heavy with clean mint. An old calico cat sat washing itself on a nearby headstone, its ear mangled and its mottled coat stretched tight over its bones. We watched each other, aged and crumbling things like the last beads on a broken rosary.

I stood over my forebears and envied the ignorance of their deaths. Then I took a redeye back to Topeka, fleeing down the map to my adopted plains and a wife who has already replaced me, to live out my days with a sky in every corner.

AN ENDING (ASCENT)

I watch the photos surface and fade across the wall. They are like a balm but I don't know if I want to be here when Terry comes out of my bedroom, buttoning his pants, my wife drying on him. It's already too easy a thing to hate Caithlin. I've been fighting it ever since the Amaranth Mandate. I get these thoughts, my hands with their first liver spots wrapped around her neck, wringing out all the millennia. See where immortality gets her then. That there's another man warming my bed only pushes me farther out on the ledge.

Terry, tall and wiry as his brother. I remember him best as a boy of seven crying tracks through the dirt on his cheeks, hurling his baseball glove because we wouldn't let him play left field when one of the guys didn't show. He'd sit on the fringe of chalk dust and make a keening siren noise until his older brother Tex, who was inseparable from me back then, would finally threaten him home. We were ten, eleven, practically men on all those fine summer afternoons. Nobody knowing how tremendously lucky Terry was, that even then the rest of us stood, leaning forward with our hands on our thighs, shouting at the batters, on the wrong side of New Year's Day, 1980.

Another photo of my grandson surfaces across the wall. James raises his face to the camera, the sun winking peach and lemon off the lens, his smile so bright against the deep burnish of his skin. His sand-clotted hands hold a plastic shovel and pail. I try to make what I see in his eyes worth all this. Then the series ends and the image changes to Caithlin and me last Christmas, reindeer on our matching sweaters and, for two more months, the same future in our matching eyes.

Amaranth was introduced in the spring of '33. Exactly two millennia after the death of Christ, an irony epic enough to tremble the earth beneath its weight. Folks still talk about how the social feeds were overwhelmed, global servers crashing for the first time in decades, whoops of raucous joy even on streets as isolated as ours. The pure delirium of it. The day history lost us from its clutches.

Caithlin's tether book sits on the coffee table, birthing headlines in its sleep. PONCETECH CEO DISCUSSES BAP MANDATE and SUICIDE RATE FALLS 22% WITH AGE THERAPY glimmer in the air above the screensaver before I knock the book to the floor. Chalk it up to more of Dr. Hinton's dissociation.

Last month the US Bureau of Age and Population released three years of clinical findings and five more of rollout statistics, but I haven't made it past the second of its thousand-plus pages. We all know the gist of it by now, and I'd already let Caithlin talk me into renting space on a shrink's couch, where I memorize the texture of the ceiling in the gulfs of silence while the doctor sits in his early forties glow.

I only know what I learned of gene and cell research before the Mandate—what some of us call the Age Cleansing—was announced in February, when my mind snapped shut like a bear trap on it all. Before we millions were sent to pasture. How from the moment of birth, humans have always been clocks winding down. The disintegration of DNA. The Prometheuses, those Titans in lab coats, isolated the telomere nucleotides that protect the ends of chromosomes. Replicated them, synthesized them, coated them with genetic chain mail. And now they can replenish them without end. They've pressed their lips to the Holy Grail and drunk deep, slurping like children with sippy cups. Then crushed the chalice in sudden, Olympian fists.

The important cells no longer die. Perpetual life. And that's to say nothing of age reversal and genetic regeneration on the horizon. Or hybrid nanotechnology, which was put on the back burner once Amaranth hit its stride in clinical trials. Still, they claim brain transplants are less than sixty years from coming into vogue. Sooner rather than later mortal injuries will need little more than Band-Aids. It's Greek to me. I just round it up to an even forever.

By the time they unlock enough of those mysteries to do away with the Mandate, we Preemies will be gone, swept into the dustbin. A theft before the gift is given. I cannot come to terms with it, no matter how many pills or perspective exercises Dr. Hinton pushes on me. I cannot because I had all those years of star-flung vistas in my eyes. The gleam of expectance.

The whole of humanity locked itself away at home to avoid car crashes and the bad parts of towns. Violent crime became a magnified sin. We reassessed the sanctity of life as we waited for the richest to line up for Amaranth, then the richer, then the rich. Until at last Joe Q. Public could sign up for the future. Tap on God's shoulder.

Then came the Age Line. Anyone born before January 1, 1980, was told the rusting tracks ahead have a terminus. A ticket punched by the BAP. Some line in the biological sand has been crossed and our genes have no way back to the tide of progress. Many of us closer to the Line could be receptive to Amaranth, but we are forced into retirement and grief counseling. The youngest of us do have twenty years or so left—maybe a little more, if a new miracle shot comes out and the air gets cleaner, like they say it will—but it is a terrible long time for a deathbed.

I try to clear my head as Caithlin and Terry come into the room behind me, their eyes stirring the hairs on the back of my neck. This rage is an encompassing gravity, like stepping onto some bloated planet I will never see. It is a black wash of hurt with no possible container.

There comes the faint squeak of her feet on the floorboards, her hand on my shoulder. "John." She says it with the voice she used for Junior when he'd hurt himself playing. I stare at the video wall like a semblance of a man, something carved from the veins of the limited earth, a dark marble. And I picture those gravestones again, Caithlin visits regularly and stands with her coat pulled around her, chin tucked down into the collar against the wind. It is always the blade edge of winter in the image. The shape of my name, here lies John Marchbanks, Sr., still with its rough contour as though the chisel has just left the stone. She will not come to see me for long, and what is long for her, anyway? She was born in the fall harvest of 1982.

"John," Caithlin says again. Her hand slides up to my neck. I've tried to be happy for all my own, but how unfair it is, that I was born just thirty-eight days too soon—less than a moment for her, like plucking lint from her sleeve. Caithlin, dean of her school for two decades and untold more, still with all her lovely grace, stern hazel eyes and silver threading through her hair like ore in red clay. She wears her first wrinkles as hard-earned trophies now. I can't imagine how she could stand to watch my face wither alone.

I don't turn around. I won't. Terry, dawdling, finally clears his throat and leaves, the front door clunking shut behind him.

"We should talk, honey," she says. "This is hard for me, too."

"Honey," I whisper. "Honey." I will not turn around. Her hand falls away and a moment later it opens the same door to follow her lover into the blank day.

It's good that I don't keep liquor in the house. My father's old service Glock, which lies across my thigh, might not mix well with drink. I sit in my recliner watching James on the beach, thinking of the day I met Caithlin, the first morning of seventh grade, how even then she constantly tucked her curls behind her ears. Half a lifetime of her cycles through my mind, the better and the worse, till death do us part.

Junior lets himself into the kitchen through the carport, whistling out of tune. He rummages in the kitchen for a minute. I tuck the gun in a pocket and drag myself away from the photographs fading slow and already wistful from the wall.

"Hi, Pop," he says, sticking a cup of leftover coffee in the microwave. He's got a good six inches on me—I'm sure he thanks his mother for that—and his hair's getting longer and longer. His badge gleams from his hip, reminding me of my own father when he'd come home from his rounds and swap the badge for his creased Bible.

"Nice of you to drop in," I say. It's the first time I've spoken to him in I'm not sure how many days. I walk over to the window and look out over the wedge of backyard. The grass around Caithlin's garden is matted into whorls like thumbprints. The sky has nothing in it.

"I dropped James off at soccer practice with Nasim's parents," he says, "and I thought I'd see if Mom wanted to go. She said you were up in Vermont visiting Grandma and Grandpa."

"I came back early. I did my remembering and I did my expecting." A hawk appears and I watch it ride thermals out on the bleached rim of the morning, a thought breaking open that I now share more with the hawk than with my son. It thins a man's blood to let the mind go into certain truths.

"You want to ride over and watch him with me? He'd love that."

I go on staring out the window for what must be a full minute, trying to focus on the hawk but thinking of James's other grandparents, young and wealthy enough to get Amaranth over a year ago.

Junior puts his arm across my shoulders. "Dad," he says, "you're still keeping your appointments, right?"

I wave him off without turning. "Yes, yes, I never miss a chance to get talked down to. Doc says I'm moving into the acceptance phase. Like this is just some disease and the anger's over and done with. All this isn't right, Junior. I'm not even allowed to be tested for Amaranth. I asked Dr. Hinton what's it matter, then, if I die this Thanksgiving or ten years from now?"

"Dad, you—"

"Don't 'Dad' me. You're forty. You mean to say you'll remember me when you're a thousand and forty, when you're on some far off planet with your alien concubines and android butler?"

"Pop, please. It's not like that." Junior sighs and sits down at the table. "There are ten billion people and not enough of anything for most of them. The climate's hanging on by a thread. Land's shrinking. They're rushing global birth regulations into place, but still they'd let you have this if the age of your genetic material could accept it. It's not like

China where the age cap's an arbitrary fifty. No one can do anything. I'm losing my father, you know. James is losing his Papa."

"'Not like that.' How do you know what it'll be like?" Now I do turn around and face him, on the verge of shouting. "You get to be your own ancestor. You won't remember yourself as the kid who believed in Santa until he was nine years old. Or breaking your wrist the same day I took off your training wheels. And you won't remember *me*, not when your brain's plugged into some cosmos or other. Don't act like you will, John, to hell with you."

"I'm still just a person, though, like anyone. I love you, Pop. You're a part of me and I'll have you with me wherever I go. For however long. You told me that was important to you."

"Just let an old man die in peace."

I take his cup out of the microwave and pour the coffee in the sink. Press number 4 on the brew reservoir and the sound of beans grinding drowns my son out of my heart long enough for me to leave, light out for anywhere I don't have to look at the magnificent joy none of them can quite hide in their eyes.

I walk along the shoulder of Arden Road, away from town, seeking a calm that pulls like a magnet at the iron in my veins. A perfect Saturday morning, Kansas in early August, drawing heat into itself to bake the day into blindness. I listen to the shushed drone of an airplane drawn across the stretched white canvas. The hawk is gone.

Up ahead one of Jeff Buckram's sons is pressure-washing the driveway. His little girl follows just close enough to catch the fine cloud of water that rises from the spray. The brightening blur of memory is everywhere since I stopped taking my medication, and I try hard to work my fingers through it, get some purchase and some anchor. Dr. Hinton would cough and tap his pen against his knee. Baby steps, John. You can't let your future take your past, too.

I watch the Buckram boy and his daughter and wonder how James will think about his past. If he'll call it up on a screen or if it will simply recede into the background of his huge experience. I can remember with an almost tangible ease my own warm lazing afternoons, rainbows flickering in a swarm of mist while my father washed his Impala. He was a short man, like his only son, and had to stand on tiptoes to sponge the top of the car. My mother stood in the kitchen doorway with the telephone cord twined around her finger, her soft, dark head tilted to the right as I launched myself past her and out into the glare of another summer morning.

Out to my left a horizon of wheat hems the outskirts of town, spread out as far as the curve of the earth. I have to stop and wait to see it rustle, so still is the day, frozen in time. As kids we'd machete through the wheat like knights-errant, explorers, form giant letters with our hacking until suddenly we were pilots rocketing our ships across the vast toothless mouth of the sky. Glancing down to see our proclamations, our hopes etched across that field, the letters clear even through the contrails and frayed puffs of cumulus clinging to our hulls.

And we'd spend a week every October in Vermont. The mountains like drowsy gods dressed in slow fire. I'd wait on the porch for my grandfather's '49 Harvester pickup to grumble long pipe clouds of exhaust up Wicker Ridge, the haunted creak of its door as he emerged and folded me in his arms. He always smelled like cinnamon as he asked what I wanted to be when I grew up this year. Astronaut, it's always astronaut every time you ask, I'd tell him, and I can't help but think of that now, how I ended up counting numbers instead of stars.

Only one of my four grandparents was alive when I was a boy, so I put a lot of love into my grandfather. It is a wondrous and shocking thing, these last few months in particular, how much I miss him. And I wonder how the memory of me will survive in my own grandson's heart. How long before I'm just a jpeg of a gray-haired man holding an impossibly small boy on his shoulders? Will he still see himself, where he came from, when he zooms in on my face? All these questions that aren't for me to ask.

My hand slips into a pocket and traces the crosshatched grip of the gun, and I remember the pledge Caithlin and I made as teenagers, to wait until marriage. I waged an honorable war with my body, lasting two years before I finally talked her panties off in her parents' oak-paneled basement. The strange taste of a woman, alkali and berry, and time moved in a swift stumble to late the next year as I held John, Jr. in the crook of my arm. His skin a splotchy red, the afterbirth scrubbed clean, and I felt him rooted to me, and me to the future.

But what is that now? Roots only go into the earth, not away from it.

I could be in St. Louis or Lincoln or any of a hundred cities, holding an EXTEND AGE RESEARCH sign and begging military police to let us into BAP field centers. But riots, protests, petitions, even terrorism—these things do not rattle cages when the youngest of the ones shaking the bars are sixty-two years old. More and more it is the churches that are bursting at the seams, though not with the young. Rows of gray heads bow in belated faith, the last of the great flocks. I wonder what my father would think of them.

But maybe I really am too old, because I *have* been walking toward town. I look up out of my woolgathering and see the Methodist church's steeple thrusting over the low trees. My parents missed one Sunday morning there in all my memory of them, but I haven't been in years.

Barre Park is around the next bend. Now that I'm straining for it, I hear a faint trickle of cheers way out at the edge of hearing. My pace is brisk enough and there is no stoop to my posture yet. The sound of children grows. I pass homes and farms bearing names I've known since I was brought here fresh out of diapers. They're filled with good people but most of them might as well be angels or vampires for all the commonality they have with me.

Still I notice the corners of my mouth tick up into

something like a smile. It is a fine morning and I am in it. The heat hasn't choked the air yet and I want to watch my grandson play soccer.

Dr. Hinton likes to scribble my dreams into his notebook, so I started keeping what I see to myself. I don't have them anymore, I say, his fancy pills mute them into white noise and I've resigned myself to the way of things. The doctor nods, lips pursed around a little "mmhm" noise. He taps his incessant pen.

But I do dream. Of blue-red skies and coarse, irradiated dirt sifting through my fingers like strange sugar. Places where sound carries forever and nothing is without heft or cadence. I dream of landscapes culled from the smudged pages of books I read in ancient childhood, worlds where cities must be torn down to make way for forests. Worlds where the rain will pick your bones clean in minutes. Clusters of moons in choreographed orbit. I dream of great terraform crafts lifting roseate dust storms from arid planets, pumping our life into their wombs.

Incalculable distances in an eyedropper. Blooming nebulas swapping poetry. Star systems without carbon, forms of life stemmed from elements that require certain coding to see, to fall in love with, their skins crackling with antilight. Immense and entire ecosystems that would fit in the metal wagon I pulled through long-ago Kansas streets, intelligent moss coating spiked stones like a diorama of my grandfather's mountain-shaded farm. I dream of the dreams I once shared with my friends, propulsion and reentry and streaking across pale skies over miles of gold dancing in our wake.

I dream every night, more and more vividly. Of my raised hand framing Earth and Sun between a thumb and forefinger, one inch and one moment. Homes in concert with heavens. Knowing when I return—if—my wife, my children and their children on and up and through the spire of history will not have changed a day. There is nowhere our consciousness is not. There is only ascent.

But whatever the colors of my dreams, in their ends they fade to the yellow of amber, to wheat in autumn, to the centers of daisies and I open my eyes blinking tears: there through the parted curtains is the one star I can know, waiting for me.

Topeka proper begins here, the outlying church and a small village's worth of restaurants and shops before you reach its heart cloven by the interstate. I climb up to the left shoulder and stand atop the park's shallow rise, under the great green bell of a sycamore, and watch James from a distance, he and his teammates blue-backed ants trundling in the grass. Barre Park is small, just a vague crescent of trees holding two sports fields in its mouth. John, Jr.'s shiny Glide skims by and pulls into the lot farther ahead. I am glad I beat him here and spared myself the indignity of him coasting to a stop behind me on the road.

Part of me wants to stay on the fringe but I'd like to see the boy get a good kick in. Whether it's a goal or as out of bounds as his grandpa, just solid contact where I can watch his face caught by surprise as the ball leaves his foot soaring and true.

So I step out into the sun and over to the joining of the two fields, where the parents of a second team of children are congregated, sharing out water bottles and encouragement. James scans the grownups nearest him, his face lighting up when he finds his dad. He jumps up and spins in a circle, waving, trying to show off. Nasim's parents are there, waving back. They will always be there, waving back, and I watch Junior hug his father-in-law, kiss his mother-in-law's cheek. They all laugh at something Ahmed points at in the empty sky. Even in August Gwen loves to wear inexplicable scarves. This one has all the colors of burning leaves. Of my grandfather's farm as I knew it.

"Well hey, Johnny," someone says from my left, and I know it's Tex before I turn. No one else has called me that since my mother died in '26. I think it was the end of winter the last time I saw him, right after the stem shot wiped him clean of pancreatic cancer. He's lost some more weight from his already lean frame, his face all planed angles.

"Morning, Tex," I say, and shake his hand, which is as smooth and dry as wax paper. An editor's hand, not unlike my own.

"It is for another few minutes. Until the heat gets us."

"I don't think it'll be so bad as that. Your granddaughter here?"

He shades his eyes and points out to the nearer group of kids, mostly girls. "She's right there," he says. "And what's more, Maisie's new little one came." He grins and nods toward the foreground and I see his daughter holding a fussing bundle, her head tilted down to block the sunlight.

"That's great, Tex. I know you're proud." I have to look away from all that thriving life because for a moment I'm sure I will collapse to the warm grass. It's been months since I could shut my thoughts off without the pills, cinch the anger, and without them something else is wanting to flood in, something almost from my dreams but yet unidentified. It feels like a kind of light inside cupped palms that haven't opened yet.

"What is it, John?" I feel his steadying hand gripping just below my shoulder. "Let's get you a seat."

"No, I'm fine. I'm fine. It's only—" I step back from the small crowd and he follows. We fade back until we're nearly within the first sycamore's reach. "It's dying, Tex. I don't want to do it. What's always made death peaceful, or close as we can get to peaceful, is knowing that everybody's got to go there. It was something you could reconcile. But now it's just me."

"Hey now, remember you got me in your boat. I never let you forget when we were kids that I was two months older, did I?"

"No, you didn't. I'm sorry." I look up into his pale eyes. He was always a tall one, even back then. "And I hate to bring up Mary, seeing as how she's gone, but she was born on the dark side of the line, too, wasn't she?"

"That she was. Would've been by a few weeks, bless her heart."

I hear a sudden wail of pain, clear and high in the bright air. One of the boys on the other field—not James, I notice at once—is holding his head and crying himself red-faced. As soon as his mother crosses the grass in a panicked shamble, his tears shut off and another kid kicks the ball back to him.

"It's a sad thing," Tex goes on, "and a cruel one, too. That Dickens line, about the best of times and the worst of times. The whole first page of that book, come to think of it. I read about a man over in Kansas City, killed his mother last week in her sleep. Said he was making it easier for her now instead of her constantly thinking about what she can't have. They're calling it an age crime, which makes it federal."

I pick my son out of the clapping parents. "He probably thought he had the authority to pass that kind of judgment."

"What do you mean?"

"They're all gods now, aren't they?"

"I wouldn't say that, no."

"But don't you want to live forever, Tex?" I run my fingers through my thinning hair, stomp at the ground in a near tantrum. "This planet's no more than—than one grain of wheat in all creation. Don't you want to see what else is out there?"

Tex looks up at the whitewashed sky then into the sycamore's dense boughs. As if he's giving it some real thought. "I don't know, John. The old world—the lily-white world, if you want to get down to it—is fading out. It's in better hands now, maybe. Besides, I never even made it from one end of my own country to the other."

"But what about having more of *here*?"

"Wouldn't it make you tired, though? You get full enough, I expect. I think all of them will, unless there comes another way of thinking about what life is. But I can't even wrap my head around that, so I don't try. I'll have what's left, then pushing the plate away won't be such a bad thing, will it?"

A swell of voices comes from the field. Parents are handing out water, packing up the kids' elbow and knee pads. I turn and look out across Arden Road to a strip of stores and there like a bruise on the asphalt is Caithlin's purple Synergy. There's no other car in eastern Kansas like it and surely not one whose nose is pointed at Prairie House 8, her favorite brunch spot. I watch a ripple of heat warp the air above the curve of hood and windshield, picturing Terry's face beyond the restaurant's window, younger already just from the pure confidence of life. His widower hands cut into his eggs, yolk pooling like the bed sheets did back at the house. Caithlin laughs, crinkles her eyes in that way of hers. I feel my father's gun adding dreadful weight to itself.

"My wife needs another man now to fill her up," I say, feeling a retaining wall crack somewhere deep, and it must be the shake in my voice that pulls my friend after me. I nearly stumble down the embankment to the road, Tex calling for me to wait.

I imagine some of that light leaking out, my fingers opened into vague claws, phosphorous trailing like afterimages behind me into the crushing pressure of a black sea. In some part of my mind I've already erupted into the restaurant, but I stop outside of Errol's Sporting Goods and look into its wide streaked window. I hear Tex come up behind me, breath ragged. It could be the light, that bright effusion, but my dreams appear to wake around me here on the beaten tar.

"John, what's got into you?" Tex says, tensed to grab hold of me. "That's her car, isn't it? What's she done? She's not worth it, whatever it is."

"That's your brother in there with her." But I can't take my eyes from Errol's window, the scenes blossoming almost too quick to catch across it.

"Terrence? And Caithlin?" Now it's Tex who jerks forward and my hand that restrains him.

"Just…" I don't know what I will tell him. Stars die in the glass and for the first time I look through the window to the shop behind it.

A faint "Papa!" comes from behind me, then a chuff of brakes. Just these two sounds that should never be heard together, pillowed in the quiet heat. I turn and run toward my grandson who stands in the road, bracing himself against the hood of a rust-colored hydrogen Civic. A breath from being taken from me. As I reach him, Junior crests the lip of the embankment with a look of round horror on his face, but the boy is a picture of wide-eyed calm as I scoop him up and press his check against mine.

"James, you can't be doing that. Don't run after your old Papa."

He says something into my shoulder, shy from being scolded. I glance at the Civic. A scared kid sits behind the wheel, not a dozen years older than James, and I wave him on before the temptation to do something else catches up.

Junior nearly runs after the car but thinks better of it. "Is he okay?" he says, turning his son's face toward his. "You know not to do that, James." He tries to take him but I turn and walk back into the parking lot, still squeezing, still awed. I both welcome and fear the thought of Caithlin and Terry coming out of the restaurant at this moment.

"Don't scare us like that, sweetheart," I tell James once we're on the sidewalk outside Errol's shop.

The boy pulls back and faces me, his eyes open and dry and clear. Those eyes have all the gentle darkness of his mother's. "But you were leaving, Papa."

You were leaving. I turn from those words so he doesn't have to see my own eyes, and in the window of the store there is only a five-year-old boy in his grandfather's arms, with the summer-dyed sky throwing them into relief. There is no way for me to ever mean enough to this child, not when there will be no end to his mind, and the life he will store in it.

"You've got forever inside you," I tell him, tapping

his chest. "Right inside here. You're going to do a lot of wonderful things. Promise me you'll be very, very careful."

"I've got forever in me?" He tucks his chin down to look where my finger rests. "Forever like always?" Holding his smile back until I answer.

"Forever like always."

"And here, too?" He presses his palm exactly over my heart.

I glance back at the window and James follows my eyes. "See how it's like we're in a picture? That's the way it will be." I poke his tiny sternum again. "I'll be forever, too, as long as you keep this picture inside here with everything else."

He's confused but I watch him decide that what I've said must be good news simply because his Papa said it. As if to lock the truth of it in his mind he nods to himself and finally grins. I give him one last squeeze before lifting him up so he can sit on my shoulders. "Mecha James!" he says, and I see his shadow spread its arms out. He's getting heavier and I'm getting older.

I carry him to his father and bend down so Junior can pull him off his throne. "Sorry," I say to him. "I never thought about him seeing me cross."

"It's fine, Pop. Come on, we'll take you home."

Something has taken hold of my mind, though, and I look over at Tex, who's standing off to the side, gazing idly at the restaurant. "You got your truck?" I ask my old friend, and he nods without looking. I gesture toward the shop. "You two go on, then. Tex'll drive me. I think I'll step in here a second."

"Well, thanks for coming," Junior says, and manages an awkward one-armed hug.

"I meant to walk in the other direction," I say. "It was an accident." I almost add that it was a good one, but instead kiss my grandson on the forehead, clap a hand on Junior's shoulder, and walk over to Errol's door.

"Bye, Papa." His voice is such a vessel, with such space inside.

"Bye, Names," I call across to him. This joke is going on two years old and he hasn't tired of it yet.

"Stop calling me Names!"

"All right, all right. I forgot. Goodbye, *James*."

I could listen to his giggles forever.

It's cool and dim inside and a bell jangles over the door with an awful quaintness. Errol's behind the counter that runs along the right wall, fishing rods hanging behind him like samurai swords. I laugh at the thought and he glances over at me.

"What can I get you, John?" he says. I once saw this man lose a tractor in a poker game and then his wife a couple of months later. Most of his hair followed along with them.

"Just browsing," I tell him, because I already see it, the thing that blazed in my mind between flashes of sunsets bleeding colors no one has seen yet.

I heft one in my hand. God, but I remember the feel of it.

The bell rings again and Tex crosses the shop to the counter where I'm paying Errol. "What on earth are you buying a machete for?" he asks. The thundercloud of his face almost makes me laugh again.

"Cause the gun in my pants is too easy." I look over and try a smile. "No, you'll see."

"I hope you're kidding about that gun, John," Errol says. "But the machete suits you. That outdoorsy look."

I want to ask him what year he was born but I can see him gauging the lines cut into my face, the beginnings of a droop in my cheeks. Something in his manner, the way he leans back toward the fishing poles, speaks of a taboo. He can't be much past his mid-fifties. I just tell him not to work too hard.

The day is migraine bright when we step outside. I pull the Glock from my pocket and stare at it. "John, don't do this," Tex says, a waver of desperation in his voice. "Let me have him over to my place tonight and I'll talk to him."

We hold our breath in the pause and I can pretend the world holds it breath with us. Only the flat pressed sky is caught in the windows now, still waiting to be filled by clouds and the future. I can see neither my wife nor the death of galaxies shifting there. Caithlin, Terry, dreams, they're all transmissions severed by a line laid out across time, a cord so much sharper than history.

I put the gun away, let my breath go in a long stream. I could never do it. "Feel like some landscaping?" I ask him, and hold up my hands so he can see I bought two machetes, each waiting in its canvas sleeve.

We don't talk on the drive out of town, back the way I'd intended to walk earlier. The manicured grass climbs into bowed unkemptness along the shoulders, the road between threading out like an old film reel. I want to think I've seen this movie before.

Soon the land unhinges and opens, the gold delta pushing us into the ocean of wheat. The road turning to gravel, then to dirt, and only the power lines remain to hum about men. Once this was all like new snow that had never felt a foot break the crust of it.

I point and Tex wedges his truck as far off the road as he can. We ease our doors shut and I hand Tex a machete. "Do you remember?"

"Course I do," he says, and squints into the yellow light rubbing against the yellow land like it's all one gasp of sympathy. It resonates. Truly it does. "That was a long time ago."

"We'll be a long time ago ourselves." For a moment I wish James were here. He might have some unformed sense of this, even if his father wouldn't. Junior was never the imaginative sort, but I wish I'd brought Junior here when he was little, to walk in the ghosts of my footsteps. Still, I could wring a couple of decades out of life yet. I could spend a few of those years passing through this ageless wonder with my grandson. But it is hard for me to picture that in all this light.

I like to think that for those before January of 1980 and those after it, this message Tex and I send will sound an echo of something, a grief wrapped inside of a joy, perhaps, and carry through the cold air of space. No one will read it, though. It is a small wish, brittle and chastened, like singing into the wind, but in it is distilled what is left for me.

"What will we say?" Tex says.

I tell him. Just one word. Maybe he sees the convergence, because he smiles and nods, and we walk into the wheat.

It is not like stepping into the past, least of all my own, though the past breathes always, rich and dusty. I fill my lungs with its smell, something that calls to mind old loved books and the wooden spoons that hung in my mother's kitchen like mute wind chimes. The smell of packed dirt is there, too, and somewhere on the rumor of a new breeze are horses and machine oil.

The wheat in August is still young even as it nears harvest, chest-high, and we are grown taller and aging, failing, when as children we could duck down and submerge ourselves with just the wide sky and its uncountable secrets to know us. People here still cling to the wheat and its memory. In a way we're all old-timers. It has been a part of my life, an ambient background, since I was three years old, but I have never known intimacy with it. Not in the way a lumberjack feels the sweet weeping sap long after he has come out of the forest and washed. But I will call it home.

Tex is to my left angling off to make the first diagonal of our great W. He grunts with each hack of his blade. We push through the wheat, dry bristles whispering against us. When we were kids there would be fifteen or more of us carving our message in the field. It will take two old men the whole of the afternoon, chasing the sun down lest it put us out of our misery with heatstroke. There could be worse epitaphs.

The sound of crows on the air, thin and harsh. One caw pierces a higher octave and I see the hawk gliding, seeming almost to not move at all, like a scratch in a photograph.

I am thankful there are no threshers or even tractors out trawling. There aren't as many as there used to be. Our only companion held by gravity is a lone cottonwood sentinel in the distance.

The sky looms over us, on and on, now as limitless as my imagination tried to make it when I was a boy and it was two feet farther from my reach. May they keep it clean and blue and so wide. We pause often to catch our breath and swipe our faces with shirtsleeves. The sun slides to the patient west. Tex and I stand back to back like duelers, then march forward as we shape the C, careful, aiming for grace and hoping for clarity. The O, the M, stalks crackling under our feet.

Finally I stand in the E and drop the machete, the deep ache of working the land setting into my bones, the muscles tight in my forearm. I press the gun against my chest and think of the man in Kansas City who freed his mother. I think of the eight years I tasted forever, turned it over and over in my mouth like exotic chocolate. The idea of dying here in the flaxen light, doing it now with the earth's warm breath on my face, has the feel of liberation. A rush, to go a little sooner. After all, I was born thirty-eight days early.

But somehow I find that the number has become muffled by the wheat.

I let my mind go up and out and then down, peering from a cockpit or a bridge banked with glowing instrument dials. Mountains fall away to foothills and scribbled rivers and puddle lakes, arteries of concrete winding toward the heart where the wide honeyed vista unrolls. And far below, punctuated by two unseen grains waving their arms in childish vectors, is a shout in letters each stretching twenty feet long, a proclamation: WELCOME.

Still farther beyond, at a distance that was so recently impossible, abstract, God might glance down. What He thinks of this word I cannot say, whether He will step down to at last join the kin He made in His image, or to grind them underfoot out of plain weariness. I will not be here but I can try to hope, for Junior and for James, even for Caithlin, that it will be the former. Either way, my friend and I have left Him an offering at the doorstep, so that He can wipe His feet.

I pull back my arm to throw the gun far out into the wheat but stop, picturing my grandson wading through it. James will be old enough to hold a machete soon, if his Papa is beside him in this yellow-gold tide.

And what color is the wheat of other worlds? I don't know. I have yet to see it in my dreams.

THE BUBBLEGUM MAN

Eric Reitan

Valerie and I met the Bubblegum Man on a sweltering summer day that never happened. But I can't think about that too much, what happened and what didn't, or I'll go crazy.

We met him the morning after we ate rock salt. We were staying at a motel called The Ambassador, huddled up against the highway south of Tucson. It was the kind of place that's got mold pushing out behind the paint and an outdoor pool nobody wants to swim in. But the place had HBO. Even said so on the sign.

I shouldn't be able to remember any of it, least of all Carlyle. But he's what I remember best, every detail as vivid as pain: too skinny in his Wrangler jeans, always smoking Camels, the scar on his cheek tugging at his eye and making sure his smile never looked real. We ate the rock salt because we were hungry, and it's thanks to Carlyle we were hungry. We were always hungry that summer.

He used to call Mom "Lucy-bitch" even when he kissed her. Some nights he'd show up at the room with a stranger from town, usually some fat guy who *smelled* fat. "Say hi to Lucy-bitch," he'd say. Then he'd tell Valerie and me to get out, and we'd run outside and sometimes hide behind the night manager's green pickup. Carlyle would come out alone and stand there smoking Camels and looking at the stars. After a while the visitor would leave, and sometimes Mom would follow him to the door in her terrycloth robe, and she'd look fake, like her skin was made of soap.

The night it started was one of those nights, but it was so sticky-hot we didn't stay behind the truck. We retreated to the air-conditioned motel office, where we sat on the frayed green sofa by the brochures. The night manager stuck his head out from the back, grunted, and returned to the tinny sounds of his TV. He was used to us by now.

"Betcha we'll get breakfast at Cracker Barrel tomorrow," Valerie said. She was ten, three years older than me, and she was tall for her age. She looked twelve or thirteen, and sometimes Carlyle called her pretty and said in a few years we'd be rich.

"*Cracker* Barrel," she said, goading me with it. I thought about fatty bacon and toast and scrambled eggs. We hadn't eaten since yesterday, when we got Twinkies and peanut butter crackers from the vending machine. Carlyle said Mom didn't know how not to spend money on shit, so he doled out twenty dollars a week, which was supposed to be for all of us—but it never lasted, and when Mom asked for more so the kids could eat he'd tell her that they weren't *his* kids and if she didn't fucking know how to make the money last a week that wasn't his fucking fault.

But sometimes when Carlyle brought a man to the room he'd get generous the next day and take us out for breakfast—and for a couple of hours he was kinda nice and we almost didn't hate him.

"Betcha," Valerie said again, so I poked her stomach and she grabbed my finger and twisted it. "Say Uncle!" she yelled, and I did.

I don't know why I looked at the brochures just then, but that's when I saw it: the one with the clown and the colorful machines. I saw blue pistons and yellow coils and purple steam spewing from pea-green pipes. And the clown: pear shaped and glossy-faced and mostly pink, except for the orange belt and duck-billed shoes. The chaos of it disturbed me, and something else disturbed me, too. The colors were hiding something, like the smell of Lysol over vomit. But it was wonderful, too, and I was seven and I knew I was supposed to love it; and so I grabbed it and asked Valerie what it said. She'd taught herself to read three years ago.

She took it, and looked at it. There was something strange about her face. "Bubblegum factory," she said.

"Maybe Carlyle could take us *there*."

"Maybe," she said, but she shook her head. She dropped the brochure and it drifted to the floor. Then she jumped off the sofa to look out the window.

The rock salt was on the sill, big crystal chunks set there for decoration or something, only they didn't look very pretty. Valerie looked out the window. "Carlyle's still outside," she said. Then she picked up a cloudy chunk. "What's this?"

"Dunno."

She sniffed it and touched her tongue to it. "Shee-it," she said, the way Uncle Leo used to. And then she popped it in her mouth and sucked on it like candy. So I told her I wanted one too and she threw me one. I can't really describe it, only that the salt explosion made my mouth fill with liquid, and I swallowed and swallowed and it almost seemed like food. I cracked it with my teeth, crunching at the smaller bits.

We still had it in our mouths when the night manager came out of the back. He looked at us with his small brown eyes and said, "What the hell you sucking on?"

Valerie raised her head and said, "Nuthin."

That was a mistake. She should've said *candy* or something, because the manager's eyes narrowed, and then he looked over at the window and must've seen the missing rock salt. And so he came round the counter and grabbed both of us, shook us, and roared at us to spit it out.

And then he dragged us out to the parking lot. Carlyle had been standing there longer than usual, and maybe he was getting nervous about what was going on inside, and maybe that's why he got so pissed. By that time I was already starting to feel sick, and so when Carlyle hit me in the gut I was sure I'd puke. Only Carlyle didn't give me a chance. He knocked me onto my side and yelled something about fucking brats and little shits, and he would've kicked me if Valerie hadn't gotten in his face and told him it was her idea and that if he was gonna punish anyone it should be her.

So Carlyle took her by the hair and hauled her into the room, even though he never went in while Mom was with a man. I heard shouting, and then the stranger stamped out and nearly stepped on me, with Mom chasing after, yelling that he hadn't paid her; but she stopped when she got to me. She looked down at me and called me stupid and said I ruined everything.

Carlyle kept Valerie in the bathroom for twenty minutes. Mom sat by the wall, rocking herself. I crawled into the room, dry-heaved on the floor, and then crept onto the sofa bed that Valerie and I shared. I lay in a ball until Carlyle and Valerie came out.

Carlyle went to Mom and asked if she'd gotten the money. When she shook her head he slapped her and left. Valerie lay down next to me, put her arms around me, and for a while stroked my hair.

The Bubblegum Man came to us the next morning. There wasn't any trip to Cracker Barrel, and so Valerie and I walked out to a field near the highway, looking for blackberries like we used to find when we lived in Oregon, only there weren't any blackberries here. Some local kids passed us. One of them threw a rock. We ignored them, and I guess they decided we weren't worth their time. And then we saw the Bubblegum Man.

He came down the hill like he was coming from the highway, and the thing he looked most like was a clown without the make-up. He was pear-shaped, and his head was bald on top with hair like poodle fur on the sides—and he had fat, soft lips. I didn't like the way his hands moved inside his pockets.

He was smiling one of those big, wet smiles that babies sometimes have. Valerie put a hand on my arm and stepped in front of me.

"Morning," she said.

The Bubblegum Man looked at us, his small eyes darting from Valerie to me. "Well, g'mornin," he said. "Can't say I've met you folks before," he laughed. "'Course, I did just come to town."

And then his smile went away. His eyes narrowed, and a small wheezing sound came out of him. He pulled something small and square and paper-wrapped from his pocket. "Bubblegum?" I recognized him then, from the brochure. I could almost see the pipes and the colored smoke. I could almost smell the vomit.

You have to understand how hungry I was. I hadn't eaten in almost two days. But I didn't want that bubblegum. My mouth didn't even water.

"No, thank you," Valerie said.

The Bubblegum Man cocked his head. "This ain't no Bubblicious," he said. "This ain't no ordinary Bazooka. Nossir. This ain't your Mama's bubblegum." He took a step towards us and held out the gum like he meant to kill us with it, except that stupid, loose smile was back on his face. "This is my own special creation, the next step in space-age food technology. Contained in this here package is the most astounding invention of the age, more miraculous than any hunk of candy Mr. Wonka ever made."

He kept coming, and Valerie kept backing up, pushing me along behind her. I could tell she was itching to run, but she knew I wouldn't be able to keep up. "It'll revolutionize space travel," said the Bubblegum Man. "It'll end world hunger. I'm telling you, my friends, with this piece of gum we'll be able to cure cancer and save the whales and finally figure out the meaning of those damned Bob Dylan songs!" He roared out the last statement with something close to rage.

Well, either the man was joking or he was crazy, and by the look on his face we were guessing he was crazy. I could tell that Valerie was as scared as me. But Valerie had a way with her when she got scared. It's like she'd get mad at the world for making her scared, and she'd get this look in her eyes which was like, if she wasn't on my side, I'd be scared of *her*.

Valerie got that look now, and she straightened her shoulders and looked the Bubblegum Man in the eye.

"Yeah, right," she said.

The Bubblegum Man moved fast. Suddenly he had Valerie by the hair, and his face was inches from hers, and he was sneering—and he didn't look anything like a clown.

"Listen," he hissed. "Listen and learn." He put a finger on the tip of Valerie's nose. "Never fool with a man's life's work. They laughed at Galileo. They laughed at Einstein. They laughed at Bob Hope." He paused, and for a moment he seemed confused. Then his eyes blazed with rage, and he wrenched back Valerie's head so that she toppled to the ground. "I'm not talking dreams and delusions, girl. I'm talking alchemy. I'm talking necromancy! I'm talking the power to make your dreams come *true*. You hear me? You understand me?!"

He loomed over Valerie, and suddenly his voice went quiet. "Chew my gum," he said, "and you'll never have to put up with Carlyle Farnum's grubby hands again." And then his fists were full of bubblegum, and he scattered them at Valerie's feet.

He looked at the scattered gum, then at Valerie and me. And then he turned and stalked away, back up the hill toward the highway.

When he was gone, Valerie got on her knees and began to gather the bubblegum into a pile. She looked at me. "We can't ever eat these," she said. "You understand?"

I looked at her. There was a strength to her then, a cold, fierce strength. I didn't understand. How could I understand? "Cuz they're poison?" I asked.

Valerie shook her head. "No. Because they're real. Because they work." She scooped up the pile and began stuffing the pieces into her pockets.

We went back to the motel. Valerie began plopping the gum into the toilet, and when she dropped in the last piece she looked at me as if daring me to believe that wasn't all of them. Because I knew she had one left. I knew it as sure as I knew anything.

The gum went down in a whoosh and a swirl. Valerie marched into the bedroom and sat down on the edge of the bed where Mom lay curled under the sheets. Carlyle hadn't come back last night, which was just as well. I stood in the bathroom doorway and watched Valerie, wondering what she'd do.

"Mom," she said. Mom grunted but didn't move. "Mom, let's get out of here, before Carlyle comes back." It sounded so right I wanted to run over and jump onto the bed and bounce on it. Instead I stood in the doorway and looked at Mom's wilted hair.

Mom moved, but only to pull up the covers. "Don't be crazy, girl."

But Valerie wasn't done. "C'mon, Mom. He's a fuck. A *fuck!*"

Shifting blankets. "Don't use that kind of talk."

"Mom. Please, Mom."

"Let me sleep. I didn't sleep last night." Mom rolled over, turned her back on us. Valerie stared for a minute. I could see her hand in her pocket, moving—moving like the hands of the Bubblegum Man.

She stood up and turned to me. "*We* could go." She looked me hard in the face. I think she was trying to figure if I was up to it. I knew she wouldn't leave me behind. "We could hot-wire the manager's truck," she said. "Drive to Vegas. We'd make it in Vegas."

I thought of us in Vegas. I thought of all the lights and noise. I thought about it being just Valerie and me; just the two of us and no Carlyle. *We'd make it in Vegas.* Standing there like she did, eyebrows pulled down and jaw clenched, she made it so I could believe it. I believed Valerie could do anything.

I looked past her to the lump on the bed and tried to remember what Mom had been like before Carlyle.

"What about Mom?" I asked.

Valerie studied the bed. Her hand moved in her pocket, moved and moved.

She looked back at me, and I think she saw just how small I was. Her fist closed on the gum, but her face sagged. She didn't want to use it. I knew she didn't. "We'll talk her into coming," she said. "Next time Carlyle's gone." But the confidence had left her voice. She turned away, clicked on the TV, and sank to the floor.

Mom was still curled up in bed when Carlyle came back. Valerie and I were on the floor watching the 5 o'clock news. He staggered in with a cigarette between his lips and a bottle of bourbon in his hand. I could see the piss-yellow liquid sloshing in the bottom of the bottle, maybe a quarter of it left.

He went straight to the bed and pulled the covers off Mom. "Hey, Lucy-bitch."

I didn't want to look, but somehow I couldn't help it. Carlyle had climbed on top of her. "Gotcha some juice. Open up." He grabbed her by the hair and began pouring the last of the bourbon onto her face. "C'mon! Open up! You're wasting it!" He laughed. Mom tried to jerk away, but he tightened his grip on her hair. "Open *up*, Lucy-bitch." He upended the bottle, and the liquid gurgled out. Her eyes and mouth were clamped shut.

When the bottle was empty, Carlyle threw it across the room. "Well, fuck," he said. "Aintcha got no appreciation for good whisky?" He leaned forward, still holding Mom by the hair, as he licked her cheek and jaw. He pulled back, lips gleaming. "Good stuff." And with his free hand he began to tug on Mom's panties.

Mom crossed her legs. "Don't," she said. "The kids."

Carlyle laughed. "Don't worry. Valerie'll get her turn later."

That's when Valerie got to her feet. She stood with her shoulders straight and her hands in tiny fists. Carlyle turned to her. His smile withered. His hand lost its grip on Mom's hair.

"Looks like Valerie don't want to wait."

Valerie shook her head. "Don't," she said. "Don't make me."

Carlyle stood up. He stared down at her. *You're my thing,* his eyes said. *I'll make you my thing.* "Don't make you *what?*" he asked.

Valerie took a step forward. One hand reached for her pocket. "Don't make me kill you."

But Carlyle moved too fast for her. She was fumbling for her pocket as he knocked her to the floor. She screamed and flailed, one hand still groping for her pocket and the gum, but then he caught both her hands, pressing them down over her head while he pinned the rest of her with a knee in her stomach. Valerie thrashed her legs and screamed.

And even though I was only seven and I knew it would do no good, I jumped onto his back and beat at him with my fists. Carlyle's hand came off Valerie's jeans, grabbed my throat, and threw me away. My head cracked against the floor. He told Valerie to shut up, and I heard his fist hitting her, over and over.

"Mom," I sobbed. I grabbed the edge of the bed and pulled myself up. "Mom." But Mom only sat there, hugging her chest and staring, her eyes red, snot all over her lip.

I turned away because I couldn't stand to look at her, and it was then I saw the Bubblegum Man in the bathroom doorway, smiling his loose-lipped smile. I stared. Valerie had stopped screaming, but I could hear Carlyle saying *bitch, bitch, bitch*, like a drumbeat.

I rose unsteadily and approached the Bubblegum Man. He watched me with wide, manic eyes. I worked my mouth, trying to find my voice. "Help her," I said.

He shook his head. "Too late." He gestured. "Only my gum can help her now."

His words were cold; they seeped into me, into what little shreds of hope were left to me. It was hard to turn around, to look, but I had to know.

Valerie lay still, and there was blood. I swallowed and shook my head. I couldn't move. I couldn't speak. Carlyle lifted his weight off her. He looked at her, then shook her, then slapped her across the face. "Shit," he said. "Fucking fragile bitch." Mom rocked silently on the bed.

The Bubblegum Man leaned forward and whispered in my ear. "Only *my* gum can help her now." He laughed and pointed.

Carlyle was pacing back and forth, rubbing his hands frantically against his jeans. "Fuck. Fucking shit." Then he stopped, clenched his fists, and turned to Mom.

But the Bubblegum Man was still whispering in my ear: "Get the *gum*." I tried to take a step but my knees gave out, so I crawled, urged on by the Bubblegum Man: "The gum! The gum!" Neither Mom nor Carlyle seemed to hear.

I smelled blood. Not a new smell, but it meant something different now. My hand found Valerie's pocket, and I pulled out the waxy-wrapped wad. I tried not to look at Valerie. I tried not to think. I unwrapped the gum and put it in my mouth.

It tasted like metal and gasoline and electricity, like the muscles of a bull, and the black fog of thunderclouds. Its juice filled my mouth and I swallowed, feeling it pulse down my throat and fill my gut and spread outward like the rush of fear—only it wasn't fear, it was something else entirely. It was giddy joy and hate and righteousness, and it flooded my face and hands with the power to change the world. I rose, looking down at Valerie, seeing what Carlyle had done to her.

Carlyle must've sensed something then. He turned to me, and I don't know what he saw but there was panic in his eyes. His mouth worked silently, trying to find his sneer. When I pointed at him he found some shadow of it, but it had lost its power.

"I erase you," I said, but it wasn't my voice. It was the voice of the Bubblegum Man. In my head it was bigger than the room, a thousand times stronger than any human voice should be. "I erase you!" I roared. "Everything. Every birthday, every stupid word, every stupid Camel cigarette. You're nothing." They weren't my words. Like the roaring voice, the words were bigger and more terrible than what a seven-year old boy could find. But the sobbing and the rage and the hate were mine. And the gum's power made every wish as real as the corpse at my feet.

The room came apart in writhing colors and jagged sounds and slashes of nothing. I closed my eyes against it but could see it through the thinness of my lids: the unraveling of the world and the glimpses of the void behind the threads, a blackness filled by the roaring laughter of the Bubblegum Man.

The thread that was Carlyle came undone from the weave. I heard him scream, and scream, and scream—until he couldn't scream any more, until he had never screamed at all, because he'd never been.

I woke in a lumpy cot in a musty room. I heard Valerie snoring nearby, always louder than it should've been for a whip-thin girl. "It's the allegies," Mom would say.

The sun leaked through heavy curtains. I sat up and looked at Valerie, her face quiet in sleep, the lids of her eyes so tender I wanted to cry. I got out of bed and crossed to her cot. I touched her hair, lightly so it wouldn't wake her, and held it there while I swallowed back the ache.

The room was familiar. I remembered something about a closet and the smell of beer, and gum doled out like payment. But it was buried deep, and when I tried to dig it up, my will skittered back from it in fear. I shook my head. Carlyle was gone. Valerie was alive. That's what mattered.

I rose and went to the door.

We were back in Oregon, in the house where we'd spent a spring and a summer before Carlyle came and took us all away. But of course he'd never come. This was the place we'd landed—too poor to move on or escape. I pushed open the door and looked into the kitchen, and there was Uncle Leo, pear-shaped and twitchy as he stood by the stove frying pancakes. He looked at me. His smile was familiar, loose and wet, like a baby or a clown.

"Good morning," he said.

As the memory surged free—the closet, the beer, the furtive gifts of bubblegum and the never-been moment when Carlyle's coming seemed like salvation—I closed my eyes and listened for Valerie's hacksaw snore.

THE MARK

Kathryn E. McGee

Settling into the chair across from Christopher, I'm aware my hair is damp and air-drying, my makeup minimal. Christopher is wearing a freshly pressed shirt and navy blazer and I feel underdressed. I should have bothered to put myself together. But it's not like I wanted to be here in the first place. I'm only here because my friends thought I should get out, go on a date. They say all the time I spend alone isn't healthy.

The waiter asks us what we want to drink and Christopher consults with me before ordering wine for us both. Once the red is in our glasses and past my lips, I start to relax. After a few minutes of conversation, I'm enjoying myself, enjoying Christopher's company. I remind myself not to get attached. Life is better—much less complicated—if I spend it alone. But Christopher is cute, asking questions, making jokes. I catch myself laughing hard, looking up at him from under my eyelashes.

I'm thinking about what to order and factoring him into my decision-making. It's been a few years since I've been out like this. What if he kisses me and I've forgotten what to do with my mouth? I order pasta with marinara sauce—something predictable, something I've had a million times. I'd rather try the eggplant parmesan, but don't order that because I'm unsure how the garlic and cheese will settle. Christopher orders something with a spicy sauce I've never heard of and doesn't look at all phased by his decision. I tell him I admire his sense of adventure. He thinks I'm kidding and tells me I'm funny. I catch myself giggling, drinking a second glass of wine, eyeing the thickness of his neck, the buttons on his shirt. Now I wish I'd taken time to curl my hair and apply lipstick, but maybe those sort of things don't matter. I remind myself they don't.

My cheeks hurt from laughing. I might like Christopher, might like *this*. But I'm not supposed to get attached. I'm talking excitedly, telling a story and delivering the punch line. Christopher laughs hard. I've forgotten I can be funny.

Now I smile hard—too hard. Suddenly I'm aware of a pressure brewing on my chin. A tinge of pain comes from under the skin, near my lower lip on the right side. My heart pounds and I realize I'm getting a zit. Not a regular pimple, but a big one, a cyst. How can this be happening? Of course it's happening. I raise my hand to touch the swollen area.

I hear myself say, "Excuse me, I'll be right back," and I'm off to the ladies' room. Christopher nods and watches me walk away. I'm tiptoeing as if unhurried, playing it cool. When I get inside, I rush to lean across the countertop, toward the mirror to try to get a view of the thing that's forming on my chin. The swelling isn't that bad, but definitely there. I want to cry. I'm having a nice time and don't want the cyst to ruin my night.

Maybe it's just a zit this time.

I pull my green compact from my purse and dab a layer of powder over the swollen bump to control the shine. I'm all worked up about nothing. It's just a clogged pore. Or a bug bite. I'll be able to extract it later, dab it with some more powder, and wake up tomorrow with clear skin. *Just don't touch it,* I tell myself. I think of Christopher waiting for me at the table. *Just don't let it touch him.*

The bones of my face start to ache, and I imagine what Christopher will think if he gets close to me later and sees the thing slowly blossoming into a mountain on my face. It isn't that bad, I tell myself, scrutinizing my skin. It's just one pimple. He won't even notice. Of course he'll notice. They always do. These kinds of nights always end badly. I should never have agreed to this date.

I put the compact back in my purse and picture Christopher's broad shoulders and the way they fill out the top half of his blazer. That's what I should be focusing on. My mind wanders and I'm imagining what it feels like to trace my fingertips across his stomach. I've been avoiding that sort of thing. It's been so long since I've been touched.

I return to our table and Christopher looks happy to see me. My wine glass is full and waiting. Dinner arrives and for a while I shift my focus to food and conversation, to the experience. I can tell Christopher's enjoying the night. I feel the cyst growing and feel bad about the fact that things with him won't work out. Not long term, at least. These things never do.

In the middle of dinner, he puts down his fork, reaches across the table, and touches my left hand. I feel his palm, the perfect temperature, cupping mine securely. He says something nice to me. It's unexpected and surprising. It feels good, having him here. It feels different. I tell him something nice too. I remind myself, *Don't get attached.* He runs two fingers across the back of my hand and up my wrist. I want him to touch further up my arm, over my breasts, down my stomach.

I drink a third glass of wine. My head is buzzing, making the room around us soft and inviting. The waiter returns with the bottle and I watch the red liquid pouring slowly.

Then it's time for dessert and I stare greedily down at the caramel-colored flan. I look up at Christopher. He's removing his blazer, hanging it on the back of his chair. I'm staring at the way his white collared shirt stretches across his chest. He digs his small fork into the trembling dessert. He raises the food toward my open mouth and playfully feeds me a bite. I let the sugar linger on my tongue.

We're done and he escorts me out of the restaurant, toward my car. We've driven to the place separately. I tell myself to get inside my car quickly, to go home alone, and avoid letting anything else happen tonight. He seems like a nice guy. Leave it alone, I tell myself. But my skin quivers. I can't help but want him nearer to me.

He puts his blazer around my shoulders and one hand under it, on the small of my back. When we reach my car, he's standing close. There's no pause before the kiss. He tastes sweet and the pressure of his lips makes my mouth open. I tilt my head to one side, feeling his tongue, strong and slick. His hands are under the hem of my shirt now, fingertips against my back, pressing me into his body.

He says, "You can leave your car overnight." His mouth is close to my face. The voice in my head says, *You know what will happen.* The other voice argues, *You don't have a choice.* He only has to kiss me one more time and I lose all sense of control. I agree to go with him.

When he pulls away, I remember the cyst, feel its pressure, then a shooting pain. But he takes my hand. I try not to think.

My head is buzzing and time passes. We're in his car, leaving mine behind. A voice is saying, *Forget the pain.* But the blemish is getting bigger. There's no doubt now that it's growing. My whole chin throbs.

Christopher is driving and puts his hand on my leg. My skirt rides high on my thighs. I want to kiss him again and feel guilty. Night passes by the windows. Christopher is still touching my leg. I tell myself I need to go home now, that I'm repeating past mistakes. But my body is already responding, clenching up inside, already preparing for him, already wet.

The pain in my chin pulses and I pull my compact from my purse to check my face. Even in the dark night air, it's clear the sore is worse than before. I can see the lump has gone dark and turned green—the color of seaweed. There's no way Christopher will avoid seeing it now. My heart pounds. *This can't be happening again,* I think. *You've got to get out of here. You've got to go home.* Another voice, a stronger voice, argues. *You're too far into this now.*

When he's not looking, I pull a stick of concealer from my purse and quickly dab makeup onto my blemish, covering over the dark color. I tell myself the growth isn't there. It's covered up and he can't see it. It's covered up and doesn't exist. My reality is whatever I make it. My past is my past. I turn my attention back to him.

We ride in silence, comfortable silence, and a few miles down the road I start wondering why I'm doing this, why after three years of being alone, successful, and happy, I've let this one—Christopher—get the best of me. But maybe it was just time for him, time for *me*. His hand moves higher up my thigh.

Have him take you back to your car. The protesting voice is loud now, so loud it's shouting. For a second, I worry he can hear it. The voice is telling me that if I get to his apartment, I'll be stuck there, without my car, without my toothbrush, without any of my toiletries. I won't be able to clean up properly.

But how much does that matter?

His fingertips knead my skin.

There have been too many nights alone, limbs spread out across the empty space around me in bed. In my mind,

Christopher's body is already filling those empty spaces, somewhere in the dark place under his sheets. I look up to catch him smiling.

He parks the car in a shadowy lot outside his apartment building. We walk clumsily, half-drunk, toward his unit. The whole thing feels like a secret. The fourth glass of wine hits me hard and my head is light. I stop worrying and think, *Let come what may.* The throbbing of the cyst fades. A voice says, *You worry too much. Follow him. Follow him. Follow him.* He leads me inside.

We taste each other in his bedroom, flesh and salt, wine and sugar. I'm hungry and he strips off our clothes. He's rough with grabbing hands that leave my pale skin with spots of color. I don't mind. I move toward the bed, sitting on the grey comforter, and reach for him. I pull his torso toward my face and then lie back, pulling him all the way on top of me. My hands roam his skin, feeling his shoulders while he parts my knees, stretches my hips wide.

He slides inside me.

For a few long moments I forget my nerves, forget everything.

My breathing quickens and the room spins, playing with my senses, heightening every feeling. I run my fingers over his back, my tongue across his neck. His bare chest is warm. He finds my mouth and we kiss, wetter than before, his cheeks and nose pressed hard against me.

I remember the cyst.

One of the springs breaks through the sheet, scratches. I

hold Christopher close, suck in hard and then out again, trying to breathe normally, trying not to seem too hungry. Maybe this is something I can control. But his cheek puts pressure on my face, right onto the cyst, thinning the skin. I hope he can't feel the mound. *Don't worry, don't worry.* The voice is back. *He won't notice. Why would he notice?* Christopher is deep inside me now and my legs wrap around his back. He kisses me hard, pressing our faces together, pushing against my chin.

I feel the cyst explode.

Not again.

I should have stayed home.

The covering skin bursts and there's movement inside the open wound.

Long and slippery like worms, I feel the legs emerge. I'm too horrified, too upset to warn Christopher about what will happen. It's dark in his room and I don't want him to be afraid or to see the thing before it comes. It's already too late for him—too late for *us*.

He turns me over onto my stomach and continues.

It's as if he knows.

Silent tears spill from my eyes while all of the long-legged creatures wriggle free from the open wound and travel down my cheek, onto the pillow. I free my right hand and reach around Christopher's side, running it up and down his torso, soothing him, telling him not to stop. He doesn't notice what's happening next to us, beside me on the bed.

He doesn't notice the soft sucking noises the creatures

make. I'm unable to see them, but I know what they're doing. Their bodies slide together, legs braiding while they merge into a larger form, grow bulbous like a ballooning sponge. Thirty seconds pass. Thirty blissful, final seconds where I'm not alone, where Christopher's making me feel warm and I tell myself the creature isn't there, that nothing unusual is happening.

Then the voice in my head protests, screams.

Not this again. Please I can't do this again.

I hear the telltale sounds of the invertebrate mounting Christopher's back. In a moment of weakness I yell for him to get off of me, save himself. He calls out in surprise, then in pain. He isn't expecting the slimy body crawling high up onto him, its numerous legs tapping the skin over his spine, tapping its way up toward his neck. I slip out from under him, tumbling onto the floor by the bed. The creature's form molds around him in an instant, forcing his head inside its sack. Christopher starts to scream. His voice is silenced when the sack completes.

In a ball on the floor I close my eyes and cry. By now the thing is suffocating him and sending teeth deep into his neck. I can hear Christopher jerking violently, pleading wordlessly with a series of final reflexive movements. In my head we're still at the restaurant having dinner, asking questions and laughing together, everything still straightforward and simple. Now the monster bites and sucks, blood and air, until the sounds soften, and inevitably Christopher's body stills. The room changes, grows cold while the thing reduces in size, into a viscous pool. I stand up in time to see its formless ooze slink toward the wall, where it finds a crack in the wallpaper and disappears from view.

In the bathroom I rinse my face, the lump on my chin gone, my skin perfectly smooth, as if there never were a cyst, or any imperfection to have gotten in the way. My body is damp with sweat and I clean myself off, promising this won't happen again. I'm better off alone. I don't look at Christopher's shriveled body when I leave.

Outside, I walk slowly through the shadows that telescope away from his apartment, into the darkness, and find myself on a desolate path with no signs of life. It's a few miles to the restaurant and I move in that direction to my abandoned car, the occasional breeze the only thing accompanying me.

Hours later, I'm home, breaking down in the shower before climbing into bed where I'm under the covers, loose wet hair fanned out around my head. I can't sleep, and spend the early morning hours lying there, running my fingers across my chin. I stare vacantly at the room around me, worrying over cracks in the wall nearest the bed, cracks that are growing, always growing. I tell myself not to be concerned. Safe and alone now, it's just me. Stretching out my arms and legs, my hands swipe across the bed, down my sides, and away again, leaving snow angels in the sheets.

FIGURE 8

E. Catherine Tobler

There were seven before you. You're number eight, perfect in every way, because they rooted out each imperfection across the seven who came before.

But they left you, your makers. They left you without a hint as to where they'd gone. You were old enough, smart enough, built well enough to withstand anything that might come, so they left you, and you—you hunt. If you're perfection, the others cannot stand.

You find the first in the lab where your makers left you. She hangs suspended in a floor to ceiling tank, pale like she's never seen sunlight. Of course, she never has. Her skin is milk, shot through with veins so blue, they don't look like rivers, but rather cords of rope.

She sleeps floating in the amniotic fluid that's as clear as water. You thought it would have gone gray, but you don't know how to mark the passage of time, and it's hard to say how much time has passed. She was the first, and you were the last and are grown, so it seems like a good deal of time would have come and gone, but you've not spent much time under the sun yet, either.

You drain the tank and she floats to the bottom like a jellyfish, curled in on herself, noodle-like. The bottom of the tank detaches into a narrow saucer shaped vessel and in the cool lab air, she smells like hot custard. You just don't want her to move, because if she unfurls, she's big enough to slide right out of the tank.

She unfurls.

Number One stretches like she's never been allowed to stretch, though you know from the lab logs, she has. But her bones never solidified and her muscles don't know what to do in the gravity you've imposed on her. So she stretches, legs and arms flopping over the edge of the saucer. Her eyes crack open but they're not eyes—not formed in any case. You wonder if she can see you, if she's aware of her surroundings, and that everyone who made her also abandoned her.

A low mewl escapes her toothless mouth. She tries to move, but lacks coordination. She cannot move well outside her tank, a jellyfish out of water.

You tell yourself the spike through the back of her soft skull is a mercy, that when her eyes close, she sees you and she smiles to be released.

FIGURE 8

You find the second in an alley, huddled in a collapsing cardboard box that calls to mind Number One. Two isn't anything like One; she's strong enough to stand and walk, but not smart enough to have acquired a job. She's homeless, but tells you in a broken language that the box is her home. She shows you the canned food, the can opener, the window cut into the box's side. She doesn't recognize you.

Her hair is plastered to her skull and cheeks, thin and brown but already going grey at the roots. It's like a line of silver has been painted down her scalp, right where her hair parts. It's almost pretty, glinting in the weak sunlight that comes through the box's window. She wishes she had curtains; she holds up her thin hand to shade her eyes from the sun.

She asks if you know the alley cat, and you say no. Number Two tells you the cat is wandering the streets, that she needs a place to stay. Number Two's box isn't big enough for a roommate, and Number Two was thinking if your box was bigger...

You tell her you don't have a box and she looks at you like she can't understand. But you can see from the fear in her cloudy eyes that she does. Life without a box, she says, is not life. It is wandering, it is lost. Not lost, you assure her, but the lab was no proper home and she won't be kept like that, in the confines of four walls, be they cardboard or plaster.

Number Two is asleep when you do your work. She's tired—it's hard to sleep on this street, so many people coming and going. So she curls up in the clothing she has wrangled from passersby and falls into an exhausted slumber. You watch her a long time, the uneven up and down of her chest as she tries to draw the rainy spring air in. The day warms, and Number Two's breathing eases, the air humid like the lab could be.

You cover her mouth and nose with your hand, a broad hand made for such work. Number Two thrashes, but only a little. She's ready to go, just like all the others. You tell yourself they know themselves unworthy, that they're ready to leave this world to her and her alone.

Number Three lives in a five-story walkup, and you're quietly amazed as you walk up the stairs. She doesn't own the apartment, but rents one room of it. She has a job at the university cafeteria, washing dishes with water so hot, she thinks her skin will peel off.

But the hot water reminds her of another place, the lab's forming tanks, so she never really minds it. Part of her wants to crawl into the dishwashers and just sleep for a while, but when she tells others about this fantasy, they laugh, saying she really is a college student. She's taking one class, three credits, Intro to Biology.

There's no elevator, only stairs, and the stairwell has seen some use. Its wallpaper is scuffed in places and missing in others, but you can see it used to have a pattern. High on the walls, it still does: tiny white diamonds filled with tiny black diamonds filled with tiny white diamonds into infinity. You feel yourself falling if you look at the paper too long.

Number Three lives in 504, and is always home from eleven to one; after that, it's class, then the late lunch and dinner shifts at the cafeteria. 504 is a corner apartment with three bedrooms; her roommates are never home from eleven to one, but today the door hangs open, like one of them forgot to close it. Probably Kate, you think; Kate's too preoccupied for life, going in four directions at once all the time.

You step inside and it's quiet; Number Three isn't at the breakfast table though a rented laptop is, its screen glowing with pretty young women—three of them, naked but for each other's arms. You stand captivated for a long moment, these young women radiating an appeal you cannot entirely explain. You want to touch their skins—not flawless, because you can see the sprinkling of freckles and scars; you can see stretch marks and the faint lingering mark of a sunburn. But perhaps these things are why they compel you. Your own skin is without flaw, without even fingerprint; flawless is all you have ever known.

The bedrooms each prove empty, Number Three's bed made perfectly. A strand of dark hair clings to the pillow and you admire the way it looks in the sunlight flooding through the curtained window. If you grew yours out, it would look like this, brown with red and gold besides.

You return to the front rooms where there is a soft hiss from the kitchen. The roommates do not have a cat, though Number Three has wanted to get one; you've watched her at the weekend pet fairs, roaming the cages. But Kate is allergic and won't see her couch destroyed by claws sharper than her own.

The kitchen stands still, but for the blinking green light on the dishwasher. You move toward it, the dishwasher door radiating heat, steam escaping from the vents. You move the latch and pull the door open, finding Number Three curled inside on the bottom level, glowing pink, cooked from the hot water. Her skin did peel right off and she looks like a shell, fresh and smooth from the sea, her skull a polished pearl.

Number Four was purchased by a wealthy family and lives outside the city. You have to take a train to reach her and you spend three nights sleeping in a sunflower field, waiting for her to be alone. She's rarely alone—she's fucking the pool boy. (He thinks he's fucking her, but you can tell. You know.)

Number Four doesn't clean pools but tends to the lady of the house, rising before her mistress to ensure her bath is ready, with warmed towels and warmer coffee. The bathroom tiles are heated and Number Four finds a memory in all this warmth, the cocoons she was nestled in when she was newly made.

FIGURE 8

When she's finally alone, you hesitate. This hesitation is new and you don't understand it, but there's something about the way Number Four walks, about the way she looks at herself in the mirror and applies her mistress' perfume before she walks outside barefoot to find the pool boy scooping leaves from the water. He's happy to see her but she's not happy to see him. She's hungry.

You let her consume him because you wonder what it is, what it feels like, to have another's hands on you in that way. Your work is so sterile and you never attempt to get to know anyone outside it. There's no point. You are the only body that should exist. All others should be purged by your hand because the makers made you perfect. All that came before was a failure.

They told you this, the maker gazing down on you as she wiped the hot amniotic fluid from your cheeks. Perfect, she whispered. This was the first word you knew, the first word you in turn spoke. Number Four is not perfect. Hidden within her strong slim body, you know there is a flaw. She would not have been sold had it been otherwise, so when she is full of the pool boy's hot ejaculate, you follow her.

Number Four walks inside, into her mistress' heated bathroom, and stretches naked on the warm tiles as the bath fills. You watch her from the doorway and she is so certain in her forbidden routine that she does not see you; there is never anyone there, so no need to look. She slips into the bath, the bubbles high and vaguely purple.

The scissors are meant for cutting hair, but they're so

precise and sharp, you know they will cut flesh. You slip them from the vanity and come to the edge of the tub, where you sit, looking down at an earlier version of yourself. She stares back, more curious than alarmed. You let her look upon your perfection, the way they made you as they could never make her.

"You," she breathes, and she looks more, finally lifting a wet hand and pressing her fingers against your skin. She's wearing one of the mistress' rings, a gaudy stone that you cannot name.

It's shocking, her touch. She is warm in a way you have never been, thrumming with a pulse that is somehow satisfied. She comes to her knees in the water—water and soap streaming down her breasts and belly. You think of the tangled women on Number Three's laptop and when Number Four's fingers tighten against your neck, you understand a little more. Too much, maybe, because something changes inside of you. You were not made for change, because you are already perfect.

The scissors cut neatly into Number Four's wrist and she is not surprised at the action. She knows because she's you, and you have always known. Number Four is not the perfect iteration; number eight is. You are twice her number and she knows.

Her head tips back but her eyes never leave you. As the scissors cut upward from wrist to elbow and the soap begins to run pink and then red (blushing, you think), Four smiles at you. She smiles and rocks her body closer, and you know. She wants to know perfection before she dies.

You don't let her, but you linger long enough to pull the ring from her wet finger before allowing her to slide boneless into the tub.

Returning to the city, you find Number Five on the train. You didn't expect this and given that the train is packed, aren't quite sure what to do. You remain in your seat, watching.

Number Five looks like a boy, hair rough cut and hanging slantways across the sharply angled face. He's wearing eyeliner and lipstick, both blue-black like a thunderstorm, and you are captivated. As much as Number Four was in your arms only two hours before, you feel yourself wanting to sink against him and understand the color of his lips.

The hands are yours though, fine-boned and strong, but for the one finger that sits crooked against his leather-clad thigh. It looks like it was broken, and you find yourself remembering the sharp edges in the lab, how if in the early days one wasn't careful, one might get injured. Number Seven was injured—no one much talks about that though.

You don't know much about Number Five; you thought she lived above a bodega, that she didn't know anyone outside the city, but here he is on a train, coming back from the outskirts like he does it all the time. You wonder which stop he'll get off at and you watch, rising from your seat when he does. He lingers by the door and you slide up behind, so close you can see the sprinkling of black stars tattooed along the back of his neck. One is larger than the others, but most are so small they remind you of scattered sand.

In the metallic night air that blows up from the tracks, Number Five smells like leather. You probably smell like bubble bath and blood but you don't linger on it. You follow Number Five off the train amid a jostle of other bodies.

He's not in a hurry. He slips headphones on, feet moving to the beat of unheard music as he walks away from the train station. You follow him down all the metal stairs and while other people peel off, heading toward cars, restaurants, loved ones, you and he continue up the dusk dark road along the city's edge. You can see the bodega in the distance, its canopy glowing orange.

Although the two of you seemingly walk alone, there are still too many people in the street. Windows are bright and some doorways hang open. Cars whisper past and alley cats yowl. If Number Five reaches the bodega, you aren't certain you'll have an opportunity to do your work. The bodega is open 24/7, and you thought she worked a day shift, but here it is night, and he's pulling an apron from his jacket.

One glance behind is all it takes. You look, wondering exactly how you can angle him down a darkened alley, and when you look forward again, he's gone.

You stop walking, only your eyes moving as you scan the street. The doorways, the windows, the distant bodega. Another alley cat calls out, but otherwise the street begins

FIGURE 8

to grow quiet. Did he see you, did he know he was being followed? You watch the bodega, but don't see him enter. You don't see him at all, not within the bright windows or under the orange canopy, not even when you walk down and buy a soda you will never drink.

Number Six lies dead in her bed—her full-sized bed that is made with sheets that sport tiny blue flowers. Forget-me-nots, you think.

You sit at her bedside a long time, trying to work it out. It's not like Number Three; there is no sign of suicide or foul play. You still aren't sure which Number Three was—but seeing Number Six like this, with her hands crossed over her unmoving chest, you begin to wonder.

It bothers you, that you didn't consider it when you found Number Three cooked clean. But finding her that way fit with what you knew of her. It wasn't entirely a surprise—and besides, she was broken. Physically, mentally, in some way, she was not perfection, so of course she could have taken her own life in an extremely foolish way.

She could not have, however, turned the dishwasher on from the inside.

This revelation bothers you, too. You sit and watch Number Six and she's not breathing at all, posed so perfectly beneath the shadow of the cross that once hung on her wall. You see the cross nowhere; it's not even in her bedside drawer when you peer inside. (Lotion, a rolled up towel, the second oldest Murikami novel, dog-eared.)

What you see does not fit with what you know of her, but given Number Six is already dead, you are willing to throw what you know out the window. When you open her wallet and look at her ID card, you wonder. She gave herself a name: Tricia.

You realize that Number Three also would have had a name. She was a student, she was employed, and a low shudder runs through you. You feel sick, though you never have before. You turn away from the dresser where the wallet rests and look at the body in the bed. It is you, but it is also not.

You remind yourself she was broken in some way. Maybe her name was where she broke—you are not human and therefore not in need of a name. And yet—she gave herself one. In an effort to become part of the larger world, she named herself.

"You were not made for this world," you whisper, once again at Number Six's bedside. "You were made so *I* could inhabit this world."

She does not move, even when you give the bed a little shove. You leave her—she is dead and does *not* matter—but you rifle through her bathroom, searching for drugs, prescription or otherwise, or anything else that might have harmed her. But there's nothing—she was made well enough she doesn't need such nonsense, so as you step into the night, you wonder what killed her.

The list is still entirely too long.

FIGURE 8

Number Seven is also owned, the property of a Mr. and Mrs. Doyle who live in Penthouse 2 near the theater. But Number Seven is also dead and the police have been alerted, because Number Seven appears to have taken a header out the living room window. Number Seven is splattered on the pavement. And the sidewalk. And the park benches.

You were closest to Seven, given she came right before you, and she was closest to you, given you came right after. You remember sharing your earliest days with her, bundled under a blanket in the crèche as she tried to teach you the difference between shadow and light. You never minded the fingers she was missing on her left hand, not until the makers told you it invalidated her entire being, made her flawed and useless to them. Until that moment, you loved her like you loved nothing else. Seven smelled like flowers sometimes, though never again.

The Doyles look as anxious as you feel, but you know there won't be enough of the body left for it to be identified in any way. Cloned flesh is only a disturbing bedtime story for children, clones don't actually exist, and the idea that an upright couple such as the Doyles would *own* one? Absurd.

It's the death that bothers you and the shadowy form you thought you saw leaving the scene as you approached. You tell yourself you made it up—Seven liked stories, so sometimes, you like stories too. And even if it was true, it could have been literally anyone; residents still ring the site, behind the fluttering yellow tape that will imprint every single one of them, just in case a person of interest happened by.

The person that interests you, however, is dead, nothing more than ground meat in the street.

Beneath the blanket, back in the lab, you placed your hand over Seven's, allowing your fingers to fill in the spaces where hers once were. "There," you whispered. "Just like that, perfect," and in the shadow, one couldn't tell you from her or her from you.

You should be relieved, because Seven's death almost completes your list. You will return to the bodega and take care of Number Five. You will be the only remaining body, for this is how it should be, how it was always meant to be. No matter your affection for Seven, she was never perfection. Your long and thankless task is at its end and you wonder: what the fuck do I do now?

You go to the all-night café, because Number Three did this a lot. She liked the low lights and the way the staff doesn't care how long a person sits in one place, no matter how little they tip. They're used to students, after all. You used to watch her through the window some nights.

Once, a businessman bought Number Two a hot coffee here, so you order hot coffee, no cream no sugar, and you hold the cup in your hands. It's the warmth that is compelling, that reminds you of the artificial womb, of

FIGURE 8

the way steam beaded on Number One's boneless arms, of Number Four's hand on your neck. The heat makes everything run together.

You've never had coffee before and it's bitter against your tongue. You can't fathom why people drink it, until you swallow more and find that it warms you like nothing else, and makes you a little more alert. You ask the waitress for cream and sugar after all, and you drink the cream straight before adding some to the coffee. You think you could watch it bloom through the black all night, but this is not what you were made for.

Your makers created you to kill, built you as a weapon none would suspect. You can walk among them, can get through security gates when automatic weapons cannot. You are death made flesh, and used to understand your purpose flawlessly. But now the makers have gone and you are drinking coffee in an all-night café where the lights burn like red-shifted stars. Everything is cold and distant around you, so you sit, wondering what it all means.

Find the makers, you think. Go back to the lab.

You tip all the cash you have in your pocket because you've been at the table all night—Marcela has two kids and four sisters and you've taken money from two versions of yourself recently. You leave the ring, too, shining bright and blue under the café lights. You wait across the street for Marcela to find it and she sits weeping at the table when she does. There is a pawn shop two doors down.

As the sun rises, splitting with solstice precision between

the high rises, you aren't thinking about Number Five; you're heading for the lab.

You find the makers where you never thought to look before, in the deepest part of the lab where the freezers line the corridors. They did not leave; they were butchered. They have been stacked like meat, careful and precise, and you stare at them, longing stupidly for the warmth of the coffee you knew only an hour before.

Every single maker is dead; thirteen in total and once you've accounted for them all, you start to search the rest of the lab. Your hands are shaking, which is ridiculous, because perfection does not allow space for fear or doubt or sorrow. Perfection acts, and so you act, but every computer you interface with tells you the same thing: all of the files have been destroyed.

In the basement, there is another walk-in freezer where the makers kept the food because it was close to the kitchens, and it's there you find Number Five, slumped against a wall, fine-boned hands folded in his lap. You stare, disturbed by the idea that you forgot about him. You meant to go back to the bodega, but now you're here, in the lab, looking at a dead Five, wedged between stacks of ground beef and green beans.

And then, you're looking at the ceiling. It could use a defrost you think as the face wavers into view above you. It's

FIGURE 8

you looking down at you, and you blink, reaching a hand out. Her fingers twine with your fingers, and she's warm in a way you never were, despite the ice around you.

Her face is as sharp as Five's, but soft gold in the hollows like Four. She has the jellyfish grace of One and the stature of Six. She has your swiftness and Two's cunning. She is warmly pink like Three, and more fit than Seven ever hoped to be. She is all things.

"Nine," you whisper.

There were seven before you. And one after.

THE MOMENTS BETWEEN

Kate Jonez

—One—

I push the root cellar door and it lands with a thud that stirs up a puff of red dust. I watch it settle for a minute then scoop up the A&P sack I use to carry the onions, carrots and potatoes.

"I told you not to go down there," Big John says.

His scratchy voice startles me from my thoughts which is okay because I don't really want to be thinking them.

I rattle the bag in his direction and tilt my head so he blocks the sharp light from the sun setting over the top of the big mimosa in the way-back of the yard. The rays of the sun spread out around him in a pinwheel of hard yellow light. For a second he's only a dark space where a body should be. It's like he's already gone, but then my eyes adjust.

His red plaid shirt is untucked and hangs on him like a

scarecrow. He doesn't eat what I cook anymore. He says he can't work up a taste for it. He can't work up a taste for much of anything since baby John passed. Not work, or the girls or me. Especially me. Neither can I to tell the truth.

"There's mold spores down there. I told you that."

"That's just not true, John. It's the same root cellar as it always was."

He stares at me hard like he's seeing someone he's never seen before.

"You should have never taken my only son down there and let the mold spores kill him."

The mother always gets blamed. Without exception. Doesn't even matter what I say. I ask anyway because maybe he can tell me the magic incantation that will make everything right again. "What do you want me to say?"

John gives me nothing as he turns away and walks toward the back of the house.

It wasn't mold that killed my baby. I'm sure of that, but there's no way I can make sense of what did.

I put the cement block on the cellar door to keep the wind from catching it and making it bang and carry the sack to the kitchen to make a dinner nobody wants to eat—

—Two—

When I pull my car into the driveway after work, I'm in the mood to sit down and prop my feet up, but I have plenty else to do, dinner and laundry and about fifty other things I'm not going to get done. There's a lot more work to do since Big John left. Nobody blames him for leaving. Not everyone is brave. I'm not brave either but I don't know what else to do.

When I step out of the car, something feels wrong with the air. It's hot but has a heaviness to it like a storm is coming up. It whistles by my ear. I listen to it rattle the dried seed pods on the mimosa tree for a minute until the fact that I don't hear the girls smashes into me.

When the other noise rises from the ground it is how I imagine rocks sound when they grind against each other in an earthquake. It's a growl but also a feeling. The sound is coming from the root cellar. It shakes all through my body.

I run with all I've got tripping over the cracks in the asphalt but not falling. All the while I'm remembering when Joelle and Nicky were little they liked to play in the root cellar with the pill bugs and the candles and the canned goods. They are just fine, I tell myself over and over as though the words will make it so. It's the coolest place around in the summer. They're just fine, just fine, just fine. It wasn't mold from the root cellar that killed Baby John no matter what Big John says. They are fine.

I almost fall over the cement block that holds the cellar door closed. It's laying at the base of the mimosa tree like someone strong tossed it aside. When I grab the handle my hands are shaking so hard I can barely hold on, but I manage somehow. I throw open the door.

"What are you doing down there?" I yell at Joelle "What's that noise?"

Joelle's mouth is set in a hard line the way she used to

do when she was little and I made her sit in the corner. She doesn't answer me.

"Don't make me punish you," I say as she walks up the dirt steps. She has a confidence she didn't have before and a light in her eyes that no punishment can touch.

Nicky smiles and smiles as she climbs up the stairs behind her sister. She looks me right in the eye.

"What was that noise?" I scream at them. "You answer me now. Right now."

Nicky turns her smile on me and says, "I didn't hear a noise." Her voice is changed. It is deep and rumbling just like the sound from the root cellar.

There'd been a moment when Baby John was warm and pink even when his little chest wasn't rising and falling. It seemed like everything would be easy and fine, but then his lips turned blue. A deep unmistakable blue. The only other time I've been as scared as now was when I saw for myself there was no escaping what happened to Baby John. That's not something a mother can share with anyone else. That's not a thing a mother can admit to. It's not the kind of thing I can tell anyone, not even my own mother. A mother can never be afraid of her own children.

I push all that from my mind and just do what I have to do—

—Three—

Last winter when baby John passed, snow was scarce. There'd been just enough for Joelle and

Nicky to scrape up sad snowmen with more red dirt and gravel than snow.

But this year the snow is coming down hard and piling up deep. The outside I can see through the dormer window is a field of sparkling white reaching all the way to the end of the earth. It covers up everything that's wrong about the house with a blanket I hope is going to last for a while.

A little while at least.

Please.

The snow hides the spot where the roof sags and fills in the crack in the driveway. Hides the fact I've been too tired to cut the grass and put up the kids' toys. It covers up the root cellar door—completely—so I don't even have to look at it for once.

Sunday late-morning sunshine is pouring in through the upstairs window, icy blue and pristine. The air is scrubbed clean. Icicles on trees made of glass tinkle like bells.

Joelle and Nicky are under the matching patch quilts their grandma sewed for them last Christmas. They look warm and cozy in spite of the wintry draft from the star in the glass with the hole in the center where one of them threw her elbow into it as I was making them go to bed. Both of those girls had something evil in them. It's proved harder and harder to make them mind. I can only do my best.

Joelle, as usual, has thrashed in the night and torn up the sheet exposing a corner of bare mattress. I tuck it back into place and adjust her quilt. Nice and cozy. They look so serene and peaceful lying there without a care in the world anymore.

The other quilt my mom sewed, the third and smallest one, is folded up just so and placed in Baby John's crib. The sight of it makes my throat clench up. Every single time I see it. But I don't have the heart to throw it out.

It's always the mother's fault. That's what they say anyways. No matter whose fault it actually is. My mom took Joelle and Nicky for a while after baby John passed, but my mother is older than her years and couldn't handle them for long. Mama was never very good with kids. Even her own.

I wish Big John could be here to share this Sunday morning. I loved winter morning with him lingering in bed, his warm stale breath, the smell of sleep, the weight of him. He's long gone though. I barely think about him anymore.

The snow makes it so quiet I can hear every little sound in the house. Every creaky floor board, every loose timber in the eves, every squeaky door hinge. I hear the gurgle of the coffeemaker, the clink of the oven heating. I know the house sounds. But I know the other sound too. Even under the blanket of snow I can hear the sound from the root cellar. This time I'm ready.

The sound is what a twister makes when it rips through a town. It's the sound of bricks smashing and metal buckling. It's a deep dark and unnatural sound coming out of the mouths of little girls. And it's rising up from the root cellar and coming this way.

I'm ready.

I am ready.

I pour gasoline on the quilts my mother sewed.
All three of them.
I strike the match—

—Four—

The front yard grass that just a week ago was as long and as yellow as hay is this evening charred and dead. The swing set that could have used a coat of paint doesn't need one anymore. The tubes are jumbled and fallen down. A doll that should have never been left out in the snow lays on its side flattened and melted. Its dress brown with mud. A single eye glittering in the violet light from the setting sun.

The clean, beautiful blanket of snow has been ripped away in a rough circle around the blackened spines that used to be the house.

Hoses and boots and gushes of water dampen the smoldering remains they found once someone finally noticed the flames and called the fire department. Hours and hours of burning had obscured most of what the house contained. As hard as they sifted through the char and broken beams they never once thought to look up to the treetops.

In the way-back of the yard from the highest branches of the mimosa tree still loaded with brown seed pods even in February the smell of smoke and fire, burned things, is inside me as much as it surrounds me. There's a stiff blackened toast smell in my sweater, a five-day-old coffee scent in my hair. A haze of campfire smoke hovers around me like a halo making water stream down my cheeks. The taste in my mouth wants to gag me with the sharp insistent sulfur tang like I'd bit off the heads of some matches and chewed them up.

I don't know if I'll ever get the smell off me. It's probably too late to worry about that. I should have been worried that first time I heard that sound coming from the root cellar. Then worrying might have done some good.

The mother is always to blame. That's what they say anyways. I stare into the black hole of the root cellar with the door burned away. I wanted to destroy it. End it for good, but instead I've opened the gate. Thrown it wide.

I climb down from the tree.

The sound is rumbling and bubbling up from the root cellar like pitch, spreading north south east and west, up down and all the other directions that people haven't discovered yet to the edges of the burned up yard and beyond to the fields of pristine snow-covered land and into the darkening sky.

I know in my heart it won't do any good.

I run anyways—

—Five—

They're going to say I'm to blame. Mothers always are, but I have only done what anyone would.

I slide into my seat on the Amtrak. I bought the farthest ticket I could afford. I never even heard the name of the town I chose for a destination. I can't imagine myself there. I can't imagine a time when all the tragedy is behind me. I fear the bad thing from the root cellar will be waiting for me when I reach my destination. For a little while at least, I can let my mind be empty.

For now, I don't have to explain myself or talk at all. I am completely silent. It's best that way. All I have to do is sit in my seat and ride. I don't have to work or care for anyone or pay any bills. I don't have to cut the grass or put up the toys. I don't have to lock up the cellar door to keep my kids safe. All that is behind me.

I'm hanging for a moment. The train's hum lures me into a calm that can never be matched in the place departed or the place yet to come. I'm suspended in this moment between. One foot is lifted, and the other has yet to fall.

I wish it would last forever.

I stare out the window as the sun beats down on the day-old snow and it melts away. Nothing beautiful ever lasts for long. Ratty corn stalks and turned up sorghum fields stinking of manure fly by the window. Crumbled down towns and miles and miles of electrical wire loop from pole to pole as the train churns on away from my house, from the burned up door, from the root cellar.

A lady as old as my mother sits in seat 3D. She probably wishes she'd asked for the window seat. She leans on the arm rest more than she should and looks out my window. She smells of dishwashing soap and Dollar Store hairspray which aren't the worst smells ever.

Hour after hour passes. The light fades leaving a deep blue smear across my window. I don't sleep. I don't want to leave the safety of the train and travel to whatever world sleeping takes me to. I've been to that place too many nights. It's no place I ever want to go again.

The lady next to me snores. Her head tilts at an uncomfortable-looking angle. I think about nudging her so she won't wake up with a crick in her neck, but that's not my business. My legs would be stiff if I moved them. It's easy not to. I just have to sit in my seat and ride. There's not one other single thing I have left to do.

When daylight returns I'm relieved to see the rusty tractors and dusty strip mall shops flying by as if everything is just as normal as it should be.

The train pulls up to a block of cement with a boxy station building beside it.

The old lady gets stiffly to her feet. She looks at me like she expects me to get up too.

I'm not going to move from the train for any reason. I'm not going to speak.

The lady looks at me with sad knowing eyes. She doesn't know though. There's no way she can.

I watch through the window as passengers shuffle off and walk across the platform to the station. The lady who was sitting next to me is the last one through the door.

Time seems to be moving unnaturally slow. I miss the hum that lets me know I'm suspended between what happened before and what's coming up. I miss it more than I've ever missed anything.

The lady comes back out through the door carrying a

cardboard tray from a restaurant. She's the last one again. She walks stiffly like my mother used to do when her hip bothered her. She climbs up the steps and onto the train. I lose sight of her.

A whistle blows. The train lurches forward. The wheels rumble under the floor.

I am so relieved I exhale a breath I didn't know I was holding.

The lady makes her way down the aisle holding the backs of chairs. She's balancing the tray with two take-out coffee cups and something wrapped in waxy tissue paper. She smiles when she sees me.

It's that kind of smile my mama used when she knew already what I was up to. My heart thumps and I grab the arms of my seat.

The lady sits down with an *umph*. She hands me a cup and one of the sandwiches.

"Go ahead. You must be hungry."

"Thank you," I say before I realize what I've done.

My mouth hangs open. I've spoken. I've broken the spell. It can find me now.

The woman lowers the tray on the seat in front of her and places her breakfast on it. She turns to me smiling the wicked smile Nicky wore as she came up from the root cellar that day.

"Do you have any pictures of your kids?" Her voice is deep and full of vibration. Her eyes are as dead as Joelle's and her skin is as tissue paper white as dead baby John's.

The rumble comes up through the rails, through the floor, the seat and into me.

All kinds of filth comes spilling out with words I never intended to say, like cockroaches from a kitchen drawer. I grab whatever I can and hold on. A bad storm is coming and I don't have a root cellar to go to.

I was sure I had a little more time before the bad thing caught up.

I was wrong—

THEY ARE PASSING BY WITHOUT TURNING

Helen Marshall

1. Nothing Hinders

They kept the petrified hand of the Archangel in a reliquary at the top of the mountain. Lenka had seen its misshapen form, a glossy yellowish-white the colour of teeth. It was mounted on a gold pedestal beneath a dull glass dome. The reliquary was shoddily made, but Lenka wasn't to know. She had never been to the capital where finer things were crafted. Nor had she ever asked how the chapel had come by the hand of the Archangel. She had never needed to. There were stories enough and plenty. The Adversary had cut it free during the Great War, and it had fallen to the earth, a shooting star, the first good thing to seed the soil. Or perhaps there had never been such a War. It had been a game of chance the two of them played. The Archangel had pared off a joint away himself so they might toss knucklebones, but the Adversary had said, "No, my friend, cut a little higher; let us play properly if we are to play at all."

It had been old Oto Hladky, the chaplain, who had told Lenka these stories. The mountain belonged to him as much as any mountain could belong to any man. His legs were knobbly like a chicken's, more gristle than meat, but he wore climbing knickers under his cassock, performed the Mass in heavy-soled boots that thumped against the stone floor of the chapel. When the weather was good, he would shorten his sermon and urge the congregation outdoors. There were other ways to pray, he had told her once, eyes twinkling. Better ways. Many of the villagers climbed the mountain only on Sundays, but the spring of her fifteenth birthday, Lenka went every day. She loved to look at the hand of the Archangel, what a thing it was! Sometimes when she pressed her palm to the glass, she fancied she saw the slim fingers twitching as if they were tired of remaining untouched for so long.

The climb up the mountain could be dangerous. Lenka's mother always warned her to be careful. "Oh, you worry so much!" her father laughed. "Our Lenka is like a goat! I swear her feet are cloven." And then he would wink: "This isn't the capital, you know." Lenka had never been to the capital herself. She knew only what everyone else knew, that it was very beautiful there, but that it wasn't safe, and hadn't been for many years. Lenka's mother had come from the capital.

She never spoke about it except to say, "Yes, yes, that's all true as far as it goes, except not exactly. I can't explain." Sometimes, if her mother had a taste of schnapps, she would speak softly about the prisons and the persecutions, wire taps, the occupation, how the tanks had squatted on the plaza like hideous toads. But even then she would add: "I was happy there for a while." And she would rub the scar that seamed her left cheek from nose to chin.

The villagers learned about the state visit barely a day before the minister arrived. They had only the one radio, and its signal wasn't good. Sometimes it played a tinny sort of music, but mostly it perched silently in the corner of the Mrs. Nemcek's sitting room. But they had been lucky. They had heard. They could prepare. Lenka dressed in her finest clothes, a red frock with matching ribbons for her hair. She was not a beautiful girl, not yet. She was lean and gangly, with a long nose and eyes that opened wider than they ought to when she smiled, which was often. When she grew older she would be called striking, but no, even the fine red frock could not make her beautiful. "What will the minister be like? Will he be very handsome?" she asked, but her mother only shook her head. "Be good, Lenka," she said, "and don't gawp. We must show him we have proper manners. Even here."

The car arrived late in the evening, and it was so long and so black and so shiny that Lenka couldn't help but gawp.

But when the minister stepped out, Lenka saw that he wasn't handsome, not exactly. He had bushy eyebrows and a very fine mustache that curled above his lips. They said he had been a schoolteacher once, and she could see this was true. His body was slight, but it moved with a slow determination that seemed designed not to frighten. He blinked constantly, wonderingly, at the villagers and then smiled a little thin-lipped smile as if to say, "Well done."

The stories spread very quickly after that. How he had been sent by the party leader with special instructions. How he had refused to dine at the Nemcek house despite the preparations that had been made to serve him. How the soles had split from his very fine boots when he tried to take the path up the mountain to the chapel, and Father Oto had given him his own worn ones, and had walked the path beside him in nothing but his woolen socks. But even those were not the stories passed from house to house, making the hearers drunk with their novelty. No, it was what happened when he reached the chapel.

Lenka had never expected to meet the minister. It had been enough to see him in his fine suit from a distance. He was a powerful man, and he had not even bothered to eat with the Nemceks. Surely *that* would have been more proper than meeting with *her*. And so, when Lenka's father told her, she couldn't help but smile that too-wide smile of hers. "Really?" she asked him. "He wanted to see me? He said that?" And her father nodded slowly, and bundled her up into his arms as he had when she was a small child. "You must be careful, little nanny goat," he said, but Lenka laughed the way she had laughed at all the times her mother had warned her about the dangers of climbing. "I'm sure to find my way," she told him. "It isn't as difficult as all that. Only what will I wear?" In the end, she wore her mother's linen caftan and flowered scarf. Lenka twirled in front of the mirror, admiring how it made her seem so much older. Her father climbed the mountain path with her, but he was so slow that she ran on ahead without him. It was only as they approached the chapel that he gripped her wrist tightly so she would keep close.

The chapel was a simple thing, made of grey stone quarried from the mountain. Lenka knew there must be far finer things in the capital, that the minister must be disappointed by how plainly they lived. Suddenly, she felt ashamed of her mother's clothing. Was it not too plain as well? Why did she not have something better? "Must I go in?" she asked her father, and he kissed her briefly on the forehead, saying only, "You must." Her boots echoed on the slate floors. She had not even thought to bring something softer, only soft shoes were no good on the mountain.

"Come here, child," the minister called out. "Let me look at you. Yes, yes. You're quite a pretty little thing, aren't you?" Lenka was not used to flattery. Up close the minister looked older than she had imagined. He took off his pair of wire spectacles, polished them briefly, and then returned them to the bridge of his nose. "Well then," he said when it seemed no reply would be forthcoming. "Well. Let us get down to business, we two."

He had come, the minister explained, at the request of the party leader himself. She must have heard, surely, about the recent troubles in the capital? There had been defectors, those who wished to cause trouble for the citizens. There had been *bombings*, he told her with a sad smile, a hideous waste of life, simply appalling.

"But what might I do to help?" asked Lenka. Her voice trembled.

"Such a good girl!" the minister exclaimed. "If only the others were like you, so quick to volunteer! So quick to offer yourself up for the good of your people, why, it's just as I had been told! Life is so much *simpler* in the country, isn't it? So much easier to remain untouched." And at this, gently, almost timidly, he stroked one of the curls of her hair and slipped it back underneath her mother's flowered scarf.

"Did you know," the minister asked her, "that Archangels have souls?" Lenka shook her head, she had never heard that. "It's certainly true," he told her, "but they're not the same sort that we have. An Archangel's soul lives in every part of its body. In the head, the hand, the finger, the tongue, any part you can imagine! A fingernail, ha! Can you imagine? The soul of an Archangel in a fingernail?" At this the minister winked at her, and bade her sit in one of the pews beside him. "An Archangel's soul is a precious thing, you must know that. I know you have kept your little piece here under glass for many years, but a thing like this should not be kept away from the people. Even you must understand this, Lenka—" He took her hand in his, and patted it lightly. "—the people, yes. The common good of the people. An Archangel is a soldier, but a wise soldier, a good soldier. Above all else, an Archangel is *obedient*. It understands order, and it shuns chaos. Just as we do. The party leader and myself. And you too, I imagine, isn't that so? Yes," he murmured. "I think it is. I truly think it is."

He stood, and Lenka stood with him. The glass had been removed from the reliquary, and when Lenka saw the hand without it, it seemed much smaller than she had imagined, no bigger than her own hand! The skin shone with a dull mineral glow. "Take it," the minister told her.

"I can't," Lenka protested, but he nudged her forward anyway.

"Now, now!" His voice was avuncular. "No need to be modest!" And when she still wouldn't touch the thing, he took her hand in his own and he moved her fingers, wrapped them around the pale wrist. "There now," he said, "that's it." The skin was cool to the touch, and just as Lenka tried to pull away, the hand of the Archangel gave a little shiver. Ever so slowly, one of the fingers began to move.

"Good," said the minister. "Good. Even an unruly soul can be tamed by love."

Lenka felt a strange heat rising up in her cheeks.

2. The Congregation of Causes

Lenka loved the capital as much as she hated it. When she arrived in the minister's car it had been such a shock! All those perfectly white buildings, white like icing, pillars and curling, confectionary stonework. But when she had looked closer it was as if her vision became inverted. There were devils everywhere. They peered out from balustrades, leered from drain pipes, seemed to hold the city aloft on their scaled backs. It had frightened her at first, but then the minister had taken her hand in his—her hand was so small!—he had said that every city was like that, full of hidden things, things no one else saw, and it was good that she saw them. It made her special.

Now Lenka was older. Ten years had passed while she remained in the capital. Her hips were round, rounder than they had been as a girl of fifteen when exertion had kept them trim and muscled. She was handsomer than she had been then too, but there were faint creases that radiated from her mouth, fault lines in her smile. If the minister noticed these, he never said. As she slipped into bed beside him, she tried to fix this in her mind, tried to remember these small kindnesses of his. His body was soft and crumpled in sleep, and she took him in her hand, gently, tenderly. He had nightmares sometimes. He would moan. This calmed him.

Outside the minister's bedroom the streets were noiseless, emptied by the curfew. It was still too early for traffic and too hot for rain. The pavement, when she had glanced it from the window, shivered in the heat and threw off the mirage of water. The city was dreaming of rain, but it would be weeks before autumn's heavy storms would roll in.

She had been dreaming herself before the heat had woken

her. She had dreamed the sky was filled with Archangels, dark smudges moving in the clouds. They were broken things, scarred and maimed. Some of them had lost hands and some of them had lost eyes and fingers and teeth and legs and genitals. She wanted to call to them but she couldn't. They were so weary, but on went the march, across the heavens. And all at once Lenka knew: For these ones, the War had never ended. They did not turn. Silently, they disappeared from view.

The dream frightened her badly. Even thinking of it now made Lenka shift in bed. The minister was whimpering ever so slightly, she had been holding him too tightly. Now she let go of him, went to the window and looked out over the city. She couldn't see the demons anymore. Sometimes Lenka wondered if they had been a trick of the light. She stared at the beautiful white buildings and the thread of the empty street.

Except today the street wasn't empty as it should have been. There was a single car coming towards them, as sleek and black as a coffin. She stared at it, knowing it should not be there. No one was allowed on the streets at night.

A moment later, it burst into flames with a tremendous noise.

"You have to say the little rhyme," the minister insisted. Two days had passed since the explosion, two days in which the state police had raided countless homes, dragged young men from the basements and clubs. The newspapers would have objected but the editors had been cowed into silence.

"Say it now, won't you? Please?" The prisoner said nothing. "Say the little rhyme, my friend." Still silence. "I shall tell you how it goes. 'I spy,' you see? We are friends here. We are good friends. Brothers, even. Let us speak properly, my brother, if we are to speak at all. So say it. The rhyme."

"I spy," the prisoner said. His voice creaked. He tried to lick his lips. They were girlish lips, set in a daft, tender face. He was a student, he had told them. He had studied literature at the university before it had closed, and afterward had published a few poems on broadsheets that had been passed amongst a small circle of intellectuals. He was handsome, Lenka thought, but too earnest to be very talented.

"Good," said the minister. "Good. Now the rest. Go on."

"I spy," the prisoner repeated. He shook while he said it. His long fingers moved nervelessly around the base of his skull as if they sought something, a lock, a latch, to set his soul free. "With my little eye."

"Yes," said the minister. "That's it now. What did you spy? Come now, we're friends, aren't we? Just friends, playing a little game."

"Nothing," said the prisoner. "I saw nothing. I don't know."

"I believe you," said the minister. His voice was sorrowful. "You have such a little eye. But it is God's eye we must be afraid of, isn't it? God's eye sees all, it sees everything. We spy nothing that God does not also spy."

The prisoner moaned. His shirt was soaked through to grey with his sweat. And the blood, of course. The blood was red. Lenka wondered if she should say something, he was bleeding so much and it would be bad if he died now. Lenka did not like this speech. It felt faintly blasphemous. Perhaps an Archangel had an eye, yes, but God? If he had an eye then he must have a face, a hand, a leg, a penis. To have one was to have all those things, and to have all those things was to have those things that went with them: pride, anger, terror, lust.

Now the minister waved Lenka forward, and she approached the prisoner. She had done this many times before, there had been so many prisoners. And yet each of them had looked a little like this one. It was as if there were truly only one prisoner, and he had simply been divided into many parts. Sometimes she felt as if it were not this single one the minister wished to speak to but that other one, that one who had infected the citizens with his being.

Lenka lifted the hand of the Archangel so the prisoner could see it properly. That aspect of showmanship was unnecessary. She stroked the hand gently, ran her finger between the two prominent bones of the wrist. The hand was no longer white, it was a reddish cream now, a drop of blood in milk. Like marble, that same lustrous glow.

"You see this," crooned the minister to the prisoner. Not a question. Now there would be no more questions. "You know what it is. Of course, you do. It is the hand of an

Archangel, and what is an Archangel but a servant?" He was positively beaming now.

And Lenka continued to stroke the hand. She stroked it until the tendons began to creak, a deep, shuddering noise that filled the small interrogation room. Its fingers twitched. The thumb uncurled itself, slowly. And the first finger lowered, the broken nail gleaming in the glare of the single lightbulb.

"Everything is known," the minister told him. "Everything is understood already. You are loved still, I promise, the party loves you. Don't be ashamed of what you've done. You're only a man. So unburden yourself. Go on, then. Tell me now."

Lenka was surprised at how handsome the prisoner looked when he wept, how he looked as if his had been a face made for exactly this sort of misfortune. For a moment, she felt something stirring within her, almost ecstatic, as if her spirit was leaping out of her body towards the prisoner. "I am like you," she wanted to say to him, but she couldn't, because she knew it wasn't true. The hand of the Archangel was heavy in her arms. All at once the feeling was gone. He was simply a prisoner. A bad poet. And he would die soon.

"They're coming," he told the minister. There was still a kind of earnestness in his voice. He gave Lenka a look that was scared, yes, but almost apologetic too. "I'm not alone. We are a legion. Others are coming."

The morning after the executions began, Lenka woke up with a bolus of terror in her throat. She did not know what had caused it, and she could by no means dislodge it. She went to the bathroom, splashed cool water on her face, paced the length of the room. The minister was snoring. His eyes were closed. And yet she still felt as if he were watching her, as if *someone* was watching her. The first of the riots had begun. She could hear the sounds of the chanting even though she knew the police would soon clear the people from the square.

"I'll go home tonight," she thought. It wasn't the first time she'd said these words to herself. "When he wakes I'll tell him I want to go home. He always said I could. As soon as I wanted. No one is forcing me to stay."

Why had she never asked him before now? She didn't know. Perhaps it was that time seemed to move strangely here. She never knew how much had passed. Had it been weeks or months? Years? It could not have been years, and yet, deep in her heart, she knew it *had* been years. Her mother had died. There had been a letter from the village, but she had received it too late. They'd buried her mother beside the chapel, and it was all over by the time the letter was in her hand.

Reading that letter, Lenka had felt she was witnessing something that had happened long ago. At the same time, it felt as if it were in the process of happening. Her mother was dying while she read the letter. By the second paragraph she had passed away. Lenka had tried to stop reading, tried to read backwards, but the feeling didn't stop: the feeling that she was somehow killing her mother. And so finally she let herself do it, she read to the end. And what she felt when she finished was not horror but a gripping sense of relief. Her mother had died, she was buried, she was gone, and it was all over.

The minister had held her in his arms that night. He'd never done that before, had never touched her, but, he said, she looked so fragile. So brittle. He had thought she would weep. She'd tried to weep, but all she could remember was what her mother had said to her. "I can't explain," she had said, "but I was happy there." And Lenka understood her mother. She understood the happiness. There were all sorts of ways to be happy. Her mother knew that. There were the good ways, and there were the broken ways, but they were all still a piece of happiness. And it had made her happy, hadn't it? When he had taken her in his arms? It had made her feel safe, as if someone had built a fortress around her. His arms were like a wall, encircling her.

Afterwards, she had placed the envelope to her lips to breathe in the smell of home which still clung to it. Wildflowers and mountain air. And she had kissed the envelope, but beneath her lips she had detected a small lump. Inexplicable. She shoved her two fingers into the soft creases of the paper and discovered, nestled in the folds, a tiny clutch of yellowish hair.

Now Lenka fingered the soft bristles of the hair. The room was filled with the chanting of the rioters, but the minister didn't stir. She should go home, she knew, he would let her. All she had to do was ask. She went to wake him, but just before she did, something stopped her. The look on his face, that slackness around his mouth, it was so like a little child's. He was sleeping at last, she would let him sleep a little longer.

3. Beatification

The rebels tore him apart in the end, ripped him limb from limb in the public square. Afterward there was no piece of him bigger than a fingernail. Except for his shoes. A monument had been commissioned of those shoes. It would be ten feet tall and cast in bronze. Years later when Lenka saw them, towering over the public square, she found herself hypnotised. They dissolved her sense of scale, so large they seemed tiny. Inconsequential. She remembered how he had lost his shoes on the mountain. How Father Oto had given up his own boots so the minister could walk unscathed along the path. Had the rebels ever heard that story? She imagined they hadn't.

Lenka had been allowed to return to her village. It was an act of clemency from the new regime. She hoped that the past would rescue her, that some sense of direction might emerge, but none did. The villagers didn't trust her. Not because of what had happened in the capital—they knew nothing of that, with their single radio!—but because of the strangeness of her clothes, her accent. Everything marked her as an outsider. Once she'd been one of them, perhaps, but not for many years. And now her mother was dead, her father was aging and tired. His body had bent like a hook, and he was deaf in one ear. He didn't recognise her at first, but after she told him who she was, he welcomed her into the cradle of his arms. "You've come home," he cried, "my sure-footed little nanny goat!"

Time passed. She put away her dresses, donned a plain linen blouse and apron. She kept away from the villagers. It was in her father's kitchen she found herself again, rolling long wands of dough which she stretched into fantastic shapes. Eventually she married. Jiri was older than she was, but she'd known him when she was a girl, a shy fellow, dark-haired with an easy smile. He was a stoneworker, and he knew the mountains. Perhaps that was what drew Lenka to him. That, and the sound of his heartbeat. When she placed her ear against his chest she could hear it. So loud! His pulse could be found in every part of him, not just wrist and neck, but ankle, thigh, hip. There was always the thrum of it threading through him. He seemed to be stitched together by the strange music of his body. With the minister, there had always been a separation. Her hand was her hand, and his body was entirely mute to it. She could have been touching a stone. A table. She could have been touching any dumb object. But with Jiri she felt as if she was hurtling toward him, and then, terrifyingly, passing through the other side. It made her feel immensely happy and as insubstantial as a ghost.

She had two sons, Alexej and Milos, and they were very like their father, with their quizzical mouths and shy laughter.

She was happy for this too, that they had so little of her in them. Both were born with a thick thatch of dark hair, which she took as a good sign. But then one summer, Alexej caught a fever, and then Jiri after him. She buried the two of them—the father and the son—in the cemetery beside the chapel. It'd been such a long time since she had visited it, but the path had been worn like a groove into her memory. Some things had not changed.

But others did. Milos was dissatisfied with life in the village, and when he was old enough, he left for the capital. Lenka didn't want him to go, but she found she could forbid him nothing. The capital was not the capital she had known. It had been modernised. There were streetcars and cinemas now, happy chatter in the bars and cafes, tourists in the plazas where the rioters had gathered. They touched the relics of old ways, and smiled to themselves. "What a long time ago, it was!" they would laugh. She had heard the hand of the Archangel had been installed in a basilica. For two crowns the casket would light up so that spectators could marvel at it.

Those were not the only relics though. Somewhere, Lenka had heard, there was a plain littered with bones. The bones were not easy to recognise. The winds were high, the sun hard and unyielding. The bones were pulverized by the elements, bleached to a dead white, the white of sand, the white of dust. This is where the minister had sent the bodies. They had been stripped, yes, but they had not been buried. The world would chew through them, he had thought, the work would be done for him. But the world was not perfectly vicious. Some things were left behind.

And now, many years later, there were women who searched the plain. None spoke of why they had come, but their stories were easy enough to guess: they were widows, sisters, mothers, daughters. It was amazing what a person could learn with enough application. The weight of a wing bone, the width of a humerus. The articular starburst of the tibia. Whether it likely belonged to a human or merely some other scavenger. A coyote, perhaps, or a wild dog. There were doctors who knew less about the human body than these women did, eyes pinched from the sun, scouring the earth. In twelve years, they'd heard nothing. And so they came.

No one asked Lenka why she had joined them. Milos had protested the decision over several angry phone calls.

"Mum," he said to her, "I don't understand what you're doing there. They died in the flu epidemic. They never even went to the capital!"

But Lenka wore black, as the others did, and she was a widow as they were. She laced heavy boots to her feet to protect them from the sand. It was enough. Her eyesight was good. She had always been good at seeing thing, even as a young girl. And she helped the women as they gathered the bones so that something, anything, might be learned from them. And if not that, so they could be buried. At least they could be buried.

At night they would tell each other stories. "Do you remember Vaclav?" one would say. Her face was a mass of scars, but she was beautiful somehow. Honest. "When he went on trips, he would always bring me chocolates. A whole box of them. They had such soft centres, and they tasted of such lovely things. Ginger and raspberry. Lavender." None of them had known Vaclav. Or, perhaps, all of them had known Vaclav.

Sometimes Lenka would join in with these stories. "I had a husband," she would say. "His name was Jiri. His heartbeat was the loudest I ever heard in the world. Sometimes I was afraid it would leap out of his skin, it was so loud. Sometimes I would lay my head against his chest, and I would fall asleep. And then I would jump awake, saying 'Jiri, someone is at the door!' And he would just laugh. 'No one is at the door,' he would tell me. But gently. He never wanted to hurt my feelings."

And they would murmur to each other in the darkness that he must have been a good husband, he must have loved her very much.

Away from the glare of the cities, they could make out lights in the pitch-black sky. The lights didn't blink. They were not airplanes. They were not satellites. They were not comets. They reminded Lenka of lightning bugs. She knew they were Archangels. She would watch them when the others had gone to sleep. It comforted her to see them. She felt as if she might reach up and pluck one out of the sky.

One night Lenka was woken by a terrible noise. She rushed outside of her tent. A furious light was burning in the sky, now whitish blue, now purple. It was moving very fast. Lenka began to run. She had not brought her boots with her, and the sand was cold. Later it would be hot as an oven but for now the chill of midnight had set in. The wind was cold too, and it howled as it ripped at her night clothes. Her bare feet pounded against loose shale, shards of rock, and bones. Of course, bones. She tried to feel them through her soles, tried to memorise their shape so she could return for them later. Her joints were sore, her legs were unsteady, but she had a premonition—was that the right word? yes!—of where it would land.

And as Lenka ran the lights began to resolve themselves into forms, only the vaguest of outlines at first, each limned in silver, but then she could see the spread of their wings, the stream of their hair touched with moonlight. They reminded her of the marches she had witnessed. They were an army, she thought, parading across the sky.

Except for one.

She found the place at last as dawn was beginning to crown the surrounding mountains with pink, marbled light. The Archangel had fallen at tremendous speed, it must have, to have made such an enormous crater. The sand was scorched. In some places it had been frozen into glittering waves of glass. Lenka cut herself on it. Her feet were already bleeding, but now her hands were too, as she crawled carefully down the side of the crevice.

Lenka approached the Archangel on her knees, fumbling blindly through the smoking pit. Her skin was scorched. It blistered and burst open. Her dress caught fire once and she had to beat the embers down. And then there it was: the Archangel. She had thought it would look like a man, have all the part of a man, but it did not. There were heavy, pendulous breasts, a gentle crease between its legs. It was covered in scars. Great gashes had been hewn out of it, reminding her of the quarry where Jiri had worked. There were fingers missing from one hand. Its left foot had been sheared through. There was no blood. Its skin sparkled dully as if it were made of mineral—gneiss or mica—rather than flesh. The Archangel made little whimpering noises. Lenka gathered it up in her arms, heavy as it was, so heavy it felt as if she were hauling the earth itself from its resting place. She did not know which side it had fought on. She did not know if it mattered to her.

"Tell me," she whispered to it, as she held the thing in its arms. "Tell me." But it did not speak. It had accepted the failure of its body, accepted the stillness of its limbs, the missing portions, the fine adjustments to its narrowing vision. There was nothing to tell. There was no secret to it. It was dying.

The lights were still streaming across the sky but they were harder to see now. The dawn was drowning them out with its colours: pale pink and yellow, apricot, the barest edge of blue. They did not slow. They did not stop. Lenka's hands were sticky with her own blood, but she pulled the strands of pearlescent hair away from its face. Its spirit was splintering apart. "There now," Lenka whispered as she stroked its face, stroked it as she had stroked Jiri's face before the fever took him. "Quiet. You are loved." She cupped its chin between her fingers, very gently, and she kissed it. She could feel a lingering warmth in its lips. Felt a shudder travel through its nerves. She had the feeling that something was rushing into her, ballooning her lungs so much so that she gasped to release the pressure of it. How could a thing that was so heavy be filled with such lightness?

When it was over, she put her ear to its chest so she could hear the final beats of its heart. She listened as she had heard people listened to the seashells to hear the sound of the ocean. She had never seen the ocean. Never heard the sounds of the waves crashing against the rocks. And when she listened now she could hear nothing except the pulse of her blood, and beyond it, like a distant echo, the sound of her own soul thrashing upwards.

CRADLE LAKE

Jan Stinchcomb

It is the summer of no parents.

In the morning we smoke the last of their weed and look at old pictures from when they were young and beautiful, which scare us. I live with Lola now, in the rundown Craftsman she used to share with her mom.

We take off our clothes and study ourselves in the mirror until we feel reassured, powerful, far from the grave. There. We're not dead. We are young and beautiful and yet death is our obsession. We revere Amber Cole, dead at sixteen. At night we go down to the dark place on the banks of the lake where she drowned.

"The trick is not to let them take it away from you, Emily. You have to grab all the sweetness you can get your hands on."

Somewhere in my gut I understand everything Lola says. I know what sweetness is, how it hurts to look at something brand new and perfect. I know what it feels like to get down on your knees and search for something lost. And I know this: the rupture in our town, unlike most fatal breaks, was not caused by malice. It was the result of love.

There was talk of a memorial for Amber Cole but her parents wouldn't allow it. Too much shame. Too many swirling stories. After the first wave of tears, even the cool parents refused to speak of the tragedy. Silence fell, a winter coat we could never take off. We walked home from school knowing that things would never be the same.

The rebellion started on the lowest rung. Playground children resuscitated Amber with their jump rope songs and hand clapping games. The older kids were surprised. What are you little punks doing? You'll get in so much trouble.

Soon we saw that they were right.

The little ones instructed us: The lake is filled with Amber Cole's tears. Amber's baby has a glowing cord attached to its body.

Amber's baby.

Without a memorial, with nothing but scattered lies, we had to make our own road.

There was an uprising. It advanced like a natural force, unstoppable water that spread beyond the boundaries of the lake and leaked into everyday life. Little girls wore full skirts and pushed baby buggies. Little boys started walking around with dolls, back and forth, rocking them. Even the quarterback of our sickly football team wore a doll around his neck. The parents tried to stop us. They punished us, beat us, starved us. With each beating, we craved the sweet plastic even more. How we loved the perfection of the chubby child stuck in time, an infant forever. We wanted to get back to that state, to relish it, now that we knew what it meant.

Then came the ban on baby dolls. Parents hunted them down and tried to destroy them. The raids were constant.

In response, a baby doll black market exploded. All girls, big and little, dug deep into their bedrooms and began dealing. Any doll would do. The demand was so high that girls were selling their favorites. Once I saw a wild-haired old lady distributing naked dolls for free on her front lawn, saying, God-bless-you-kids and good-for-you. Children from neighboring towns would meet us in the woods with pillowcases bursting with plastic babies.

And what became of the baby dolls, our dear little ones? We held them and played with them, and then we took them down to the lake. We laid them down on the damp dirt, where water and earth mixed. The lake had always thrilled me, even scared me, and now it was alive with dolls.

The police tried to stop us. They patrolled the banks of the lake, but the lake was large, endless, and there were always more kids than cops.

I no longer remember what our lake used to look like. Tiny heads and delicate limbs grow from the cattails. The banks are great walls of shimmering plastic. It is exactly as the little kids prophesied: a shoestring dipped in glow-in-the-dark paint is attached to each doll. Lola has made hundreds of these. She goes out at night in her white crochet bikini to tend to them.

"You're so devoted, Lola. It's hard, repeating the same chore every day. How do you do it?"

"Easy. I love all the kids in this town."

She's right. I love them too. They are good kids. And Lola is a good leader.

Because we had no parents—we never really had them, even before they began to trickle away—Lola had to teach me everything. All the secrets. She told me how Amber became a mother. And then she told me how Amber tried to get rid of her baby before she jumped into the lake.

The violence of it. The fear. Blood covered this story as well, another deluge of pain. Before long I started having cramps.

"Lola, what's happening to me?"

"Nothing. Everything. It's because you're a female too."

Before they moved away, I saw Amber's parents fighting with someone on their front porch. They stood there, ashen, while this woman screamed that they had destroyed the whole town. Amber's parents were the first to load up their car and drive off.

It doesn't take long to get rid of the parents. The first stage is vacation time. They disappear on long weekends, and then go off on their own for one week, two weeks. Pretty soon it's the whole summer. They come back from time to time with food and new clothes. Never dolls. They cook and throw out the trash, watch television and ask us about school. We call this "playing normal." That was always their favorite game. When they leave, we come alive again. We take off all our clothes and run through the streets at night. Clutching our babies, we head down to the radiance of Cradle Lake.

THE ARROW OF TIME

Kate Dollarhyde

We abide in the small, thin hours of dawn, my mother and I. Her hand is slack and paper-thin in mine, her lips just parted. The ghost of breath slides between her gritted teeth, insistent still but ebbing, the slow draining away of an overfull life.

She has cancer. There's no point in saying what kind because it's everywhere. Its tiny grasping hands are ten hundred million strong and sunk deep into every turned-out pocket of her sagging flesh. She's dying, and in this moment I'm so furious with her that I can't speak. So, I hold her hand.

My mother is a scientist—an astrophysicist and an engineer. She is a clever, brilliant woman. And she has long thought, must still surely think under all those comatic layers of drug-induced sleep, that if she could gaze far enough back into time, she could figure out just where we'd gone so wrong. That's why she built the time machine.

I was born at the start of summer, of *the* summer—the first summer the North Pole turned to slurry. California shriveled under skies washed red with wildfire haze. Shasta Lake, the state's largest reservoir, surrendered her last drops of water. Communities too long disempowered and disenfranchised were made to reckon with a reality that scientists like my mother had warned them of for decades: this hot, dry world was their new home, and there would be no going back. Millions of people lost their jobs, their homes, their lives. Many of those remaining fled to the cities, and the cities buckled under the weight of their untold grief, their justified fury.

My mother was born in a century that still held close to its chest the naive belief that anything could be fixed if you could just divine the correct number of resolutions to sign, could just levy the proper sanctions on the country of time. From what I've read of her journals, it was a beautiful place. Stuffed among her calculations, her frustrations, and her many miseries are memories of it sketched in a spidery hand:

Yesterday I drove down to the ocean. Green hills rolled right to the beach where they became dunes, sand, sea. I stood at the top of one of them and for a moment felt as if I were tilting down, as if the green of the bobbing grass and the white of the waves were all rushing up to greet me in a great tsunami tide. The swirl of color made me dizzy, and I fell hard to my knees. The grass was soft and caught me.

I took off my sandals and buried my toes in the grass. It felt obscene, unreal, almost grotesquely taboo. It felt so good: the rain-fed grasses between my toes, that heady smell of bright and blinding life.

I wanted to embrace it, the coast, and let it come into me. I believed, even if briefly, that I could carry its seeds and give birth to something new, better—a child of seafoam skin and driftwood bones who would demand water from the desert with thunderous lungs.

Every long entry read so, like stories she told herself, stories that gathered up the unraveling strands of the world she knew and knit them back together into a comforting whole.

I am sick with anger when I imagine her in green hills, standing on an impermeable coastline. Sick not because it's what I've never had—even if I haven't—but because she always longed to go back there, back to that time. Or maybe it's the guilt that turns my stomach; she tried to save the world, and I just wanted her to read to me bedtime stories. Noble goals mean nothing to a child, but as an adult I think I understand—she did it for love. If I could have stood beside her in green hills, to her, it would be worth any sacrifice.

There's light on the horizon now. A nurse shuffles through the door, a coffee-scented cloud in the shape of a human being. She pulls the curtain aside and checks my mother's vitals. She spares a moment to check on me, too, sympathy thick in the lines of her forehead. She tells me to get some rest, that it could be hours yet, but I don't want to. My rage keeps me awake, burning like slag down through my gut. My mother traded her life for an impossible dream, and now we will never have another chance to make things right between us.

I stare into my mother's face hoping I might see through her skin to the knot of longing that must live lodged behind her brow. I want to understand. I pinch the insides of her wrists, and she doesn't even blink.

Wake up, wake up, wake up. One last time—you owe me that much.

When I was fourteen, she me took out West, out as far as we could go, out to where her dream for me was grown. It was her first visit to the coast since that day she dug her toes into the seaside grass, a day almost fifteen years dead.

We drove through the desert. We drove through coastal mountains barren or burned. The heat was unbearable, radiating from the ground in dancing silver sheets. She wouldn't let me turn on the air conditioner, and I could feel my heart racing, a headache coming on, nausea rising in my chest.

"Energy is so expensive now," she said. "Not like when I was your age." Our two carboys of stale, cloudy water clinked in the back of the car, crashing together with every pothole bounce. "Shit," she'd laughed, "that was a big one."

We rode in silence past long-fallow fields of wizened almond trees, their black limbs stretched like clawed hands in supplication to a sky that had long ago stopped answering prayers for rain. The twisting highway led us past towns now a graveyard of tumbledown buildings all huddled together.

She stared ahead, eyes narrowed and always scanning for something only she could see. I tried to imagine her past overlaid on the brown hills, a flickering superimposition of beryl and chartreuse, malachite and verdigris. I saw flickers of all that had once been reflected in her eyes. Her knuckles whitened on the steering wheel. She patted me on the knee.

"You'll see," she said, and grinned. "You'll see."

She parked the car. We stood together on the porous border between earth and sea. We were miles still from the old coast. There was no dense coastal forest, no grassy, sloping hill—no dunes, no scrubby shrubs, no sand at all, just seething, wild seas screaming into an implacable wind.

She stared unblinking until her eyes watered and tears tracked down her cheeks. "There's nothing left. *Cupressus abramsiana, Sequoia sempervirens*—they're all gone." She tried to take my hand, but I pulled away.

I couldn't understand her tears because I felt only joy. I had never known the cities the sea had swallowed up on its slow crawl inland, so I never knew to miss them. This was the only coast I had ever known, and as far I could confirm with my own eyes, the only coast that had ever been. It was a feral land, this new California. It was fierce and angry. It was there

I discovered the wonder humans hold for uncontrollable places. I wouldn't have given that awe up for anything, not those green hills, not even my mother's arms around my shoulders. This wild California, my only home.

She changed after that. She filled journal after journal. They fell from her shelves like water and puddled on the floor, lakes of calculations woven through with memories, stitched with a thread longing I couldn't cut. She drowned herself in old nature magazines and museums brimming with dioramas of lush ecosystems that no longer exist. She became more textbook than mother. She grew frighteningly thin, like the past was eating her alive. Her thoughts turned from observing the past to visiting it, and she spent the next twenty years figuring out how.

She built her machine in the basement of our falling-down house in our sprawling, sultry city. The machine was her solution to the arrow of time, a physical expression of her refutation of entropy. She would copy herself into the past—a fork in the road, a divergence, a rebuilding, identical in the now and then, both conscious, both her, but separated by thirty-four years. *Time moves both ways*—she'd underlined it in her final notebook several times; her hand was so insistent the pen tore deep grooves into the pages beneath it.

She built it from the bones of scrapped airliners, from the guts of abandoned hospital machinery. She built it to run on intention and believed her clarity of purpose was more than power enough.

At thirty-four I watched her, then fifty-seven, step into that machine. It closed around her like a flower unfurling in reverse. She was hidden for a few moments, only the space of a few breaths. The machine's door slid open and she stumbled out, and then collapsed. Her smile was bright and her breath short. She pushed sweaty hair away from her face, and I saw that her hands shook. Tears shone in the corners of her eyes.

I helped her up from the floor. She wobbled as she stood. "What happened? Did it work?" I asked.

She pulled me into a rib-crushing hug. "*Yes.*" And smiled only wider. Then, she fainted.

It's midday. The hospital that hours ago was so quiet now grows loud. Patients cough and shift in their beds. Nurses' shoes squeak as they rush down the halls, always in a hurry. Beside me, my mother's skin grows slowly blue. Her breath comes fast and slow in cycles, as if still deciding whether to stay or go. Her eyes no longer draw sliding loops beneath her lids. Too soon, she's still. The afternoon light through the blinds is golden. Bars of buttery yellow divide the room into long slivers of dark and light. My shadow lies across my mother as if in mourning. It does the work of the living that I can't yet bring myself to do.

She's dead, and the anger that had kept me together

during her brief illness leaches from me like water from the earth. Without it to sustain me, I am dry, desiccated. Now I am loose topsoil, and I fear at any moment I might be carried off by a light breeze. A part of me wants to believe her last thought was for me, but another hopes it was for her green hills, for her long-gone country. The two hopes twist in my chest, slippery eels in a bag, as I sign the hospital's interminable paperwork.

She is cremated, and I am filled with a longing for her touch so acute I can hardly breathe for its sharp talons in my ribs. I wanted her to ask me if I'd miss her.

Months before she finished the machine, she begged me to go with her; she wanted me to see it once with her, her century. A copy of me and a copy of her that could stand hand in hand and taste the old world's living wind.

But I was afraid, and she went alone.

I stand before it now, my mother's machine. My toes, bare and cold, edge toward the threshold. I hold her ashes in a simple urn in the crook of my arm. They're surprisingly heavy, but then, she was an unusually tall woman.

I have only the vaguest notion of how it works—worldlines, light cones, the second law of thermodynamics, and other, more impenetrable things scribbled in her characteristically cramped hand—but I know how to push buttons. One of them says OPEN; I press it and the door slides away.

The machine is a metal womb. My feet are silent on the thick steel as I climb inside. There are buttons here, too: OPEN, CLOSE, and one unlabeled. I press CLOSE and the door slides back into place. The womb is dark and silent.

"Think of it as a camera, she said, "a camera that records the unseen parts of you and sends you like a telegraph across an impossible distance." The half of me that holds a fierce allegiance to "now" wrestles with the reluctant half that wants to know my mother's "then," to finally know all of her.

I am still afraid, because I know what the machine does *to* you, if not exactly what it *does*. She hadn't known, and had pressed the buttons anyway. Nothing happened that we could see, and in three months she was dying of cancer. She never said so, but I think she knew it would kill her—she was too clever not to consider the possibility. Perhaps she did that careful calculus and decided it was worth it. I wish she would have told me, but then, I also didn't think to ask.

I want to know what she was expecting. A coin flip of consciousness? Press the button, create of fork, hope that consciousness prime took the leftmost path and fell into the past? She knew that if it had worked it wouldn't work that way, that she would press the button and nothing would happen, that she'd climb out of the womb and still be in the world she loathed. She knew also that she would press the button and fall a few feet onto a cold cement floor and be in the world of then. Both branches of the fork would be her—prime, equal and identical. That's what she believed, anyway. That much I understand from her journals.

I sit curled in the cool metal womb. I can't decide if I will press the button. I want a version of me to go back and see what so moved her, but I want a version of me to live on, too. I could die in a hospital bed in three months' time because I was drawn in by my mother's dream of those green rolling hills. I could die like she did while letting one of me live in distant light. I could let one of me watch the earth turn brown, the oceans rise, the coast dissolve like sugar-glass in water. I could sacrifice my "now" self for a glimpse of what was gone.

I think of my dusty city, my thirsty, sprawling city clinging to the face of a swiftly changing earth. Solar stills that I built bob in its bay like a flock of sea birds, stills that bring fresh water to our dry land. They water our small garden plots, they wash the dust from our eyes, from our skin, from our hair. They wet our sticky tongues. They keep us alive. But their design is not perfect, and we need so many more to do better than just *survive*.

Mine is the world I want my mother to see. Mine is a world that does not need saving. The unlabeled button is warm beneath my fingertip. I remember: the machine runs on intention. I am no longer afraid.

I hold my mother's ashes hard against my chest. I hear her calling to me from twenty years away. I smell the wild sea breeze. The burned-brown hills hold us up to the hazy sky. When I touch the button, I am holding her hand. Together we can love this world. I only have to go back and show her how.

I press the button.

THE GOD OF LOW THINGS

Stephen Graham Jones

It was the prairie dog's own stupid fault.

Can an animal kill itself?

Trevor was pretty sure this one just had.

Trevor could have been a hawk, or a dog off its leash, or even a car, and the prairie dog would be just as dead, and it would have been just as unintentional. Just as much a part of nature. This is how things go, and how they've always been going, with or without Trevor and his bike. In programming terms—which Belinda would be all over his case for bringing into yet another discussion, but this discussion was just in his head, so she didn't have to know—in programming terms, Trevor would be a function, this prairie dog the variable that had plugged itself into that function, to get processed through.

The product, the result, the output?

Death.

Well, close to death.

Right now the prairie dog was flopping around beside the concrete path.

How Trevor knew he was a good citizen here was he'd pedaled all the way back *up*hill to witness this. Because watching a rodent spasm and kick and bleed from the mouth was his just punishment for having been coming down this hill at twenty minutes after two on a Thursday afternoon, to deliver Belinda the laptop he'd mostly fixed for her?

Evidently.

Never mind that the moments after the impact, Trevor had veered back and forth on the bike, fighting for control, one of his feet coming all the way off his pedals so that he probably looked like a cartoon character for all the people driving by on the road.

He'd straightened up, though, had braked without quite locking the rear tire, and had even managed to keep from careening off into the prairie dog town proper, and collapsing who knew how many tunnels and dens on his way to the fence down the hill.

What he deserved for that, he figured, was an award from the animal kingdom, a commendation from Mother Nature herself. What he deserved was a prairie dog dignitary coming up and ceremoniously bestowing upon Trevor some object his ancestors had found buried in the dirt generations ago, and then meticulously cleaned and kept in a holy place, for just such an occasion as this.

Trevor grinned, thinking of the prairie dog dignitary

wearing a red sash with gold fringe. And a monocle, maybe. The kind with a chain hanging down like from a watch fob. Or do all monocles have that? No, not that kind that are up on a stick. Unless only those opera-glassy spectacles got sticks.

Either way, Trevor was the hero, here.

And, if he had been a car? Then he'd be miles past already, oblivious that he'd even run anything over.

So, it was only due to his trying to save the world one pedal at a time—Belinda was all the way against fossil fuels—that he was here now, leaning over his handlebars in the sun, watching a prairie dog hump and jerk and die.

If that was in fact what was going to happen, here.

It had taken Trevor, what? Forty-five seconds to regain control of his bike, stop, then grind back up here to where this had happened?

And now, now he'd been watching for probably a whole minute.

The prairie dog was still flopping.

Trevor huffed air out in appreciation for these mortal gymnastics going on beside the path, but there were no other bikers there to be impressed along with him. Just a lot of little brown heads poking up from the ground, their eyes black marbles, their noses twitching.

"Nothing to see here," Trevor said to them. "Move along, move along."

It would be over soon. It had to be.

How long could it take for a stupid prairie dog to stupid-*die*?

Couldn't some other prairie dog scurry out here, finish this already?

But prairie dogs were probably herbivores, Trevor figured. Maybe the occasional bug, if it got in the way of a particularly tasty seed. A prairie dog would never think to apply its big rodent teeth to the neck of a fatally-crushed... brother or daughter or, or—*townie*, Trevor decided. That's probably what prairie dogs called each other.

Unless of course this dying prairie dog had been *sentenced* to try this mad dash in front of this giant bicycle.

Why else would it have tried?

Why did the prairie dog cross the road?

"To kill itself," Trevor mumbled.

Because—it had all those great animal senses, didn't it? And it had grown up here, hadn't it? It had come of age with bikes always whizzing through at high speeds. There were probably stories handed down since caveman prairie dog times, about how you crossed only when sound *wasn't* approaching, never when it *was* approaching, right?

The same way prairie dogs had distinct alarm calls for hawks and dogs, they probably had something for cyclists. Maybe they even distinguished between road and mountain and commuter bike, for all Trevor knew.

All of which came down to: no way was this Trevor's fault.

When he told Belinda about all this later, after he'd explained the new way her laptop was going to be working, he would recreate the scene for her. There's him, pedal pedal

pedal, her laptop strapped carefully into his messenger bag, his eyes intent on this delivery, as she needs this for work tomorrow. There's the prairie dog, down in the blocks, as it were, front knees bent, back legs coiled, that little black-tipped tail twitching back and forth, eyes casing the concrete path, waiting for that whirring sound to come.

At which point it happens: the prairie dog surges forward in slow, dramatic motion—maybe it's a thrill-seeker?—spins out a bit in the loose dirt but scrabbles deep with its claws, finds enough purchase to jump out onto the hot concrete, to stretch itself out to its complete length, minimizing the chances of this coming tire possibly missing it.

Had Trevor managed to avoid it somehow, then the result would have been a wreck, probably. Him and his bag and his bike parting ways mid-cartwheel.

And then what would Belinda have had for work tomorrow?

Motorists probably would have even pulled over to make sure he was all right.

All the prairie dogs would be in their safe little hidey holes by then, of course. None of them telling any secrets about what had really gone down in the overworld.

So, had running this one prairie dog over even been a choice, which it hadn't been, then Trevor would have effectively had no choice. It was that prairie dogs' life or it was Belinda's slideshow presentation tomorrow.

Never mind any injury his own person might have incurred, of course.

He was the least important part of this equation.

And this prairie dog, it was still flopping back and forth.

Had it been *three* minutes, now?

This was verging on comedy. On the truly ridiculous.

Trevor looked up the hill for any other cyclist cresting, and then down the hill, for any bikes starting the long climb.

He was still alone. Because it was Thursday, and not lunch, not five o'clock. And hot.

He clocked the traffic on the road. Maybe eight cars in half a minute? Meaning sixteen per minute, at least in the lane by the path. Fifty in the time he'd been sitting here.

None of them were looking over at Trevor. If they gave him any thought, then at worst he was catching a call, and taking up some concrete to do it.

The cars were just there for a blip and gone, though. And no way, at their speed, could their drivers register a single dying prairie dog. Or where Trevor's front tire might be in relation to that single dying prairie dog. The one they couldn't see anyway. The one they would never know about, even if they slowed down and leaned over to see out the passenger side window.

Trevor shrugged his left shoulder about this, nodded to himself that it was the right decision, the *only* decision if you thought about it, and he walked his bike up to this flopping prairie dog.

He breathed in, held it, then gave his handlebars all the weight he had, rolled forward across the small body, pretty sure that that crunch that came up through the forks was ribs, splintering into small lungs.

It was for the best.

There was no way this prairie dog had been going to live.

A dark clotty red spurted from the—the *face*, Trevor would have had to have said, as he couldn't tell mouth from eyes from ears from nose—and from the backside as well.

There was a kind of swallowed chirrup, too, from the prairie dog's throat. Probably it had just been the result of the contents of its lungs whooshing all at once over the vocal cords, Trevor figured. Technically a last gasp, sure. But not a sad farewell to all the other prairie dogs watching, their ears cupped in the Trevor's direction.

Maybe this *had* to happen periodically, right?

Trevor supposed it had to.

Not because for every fifty prairie dogs that come along, one or two are going to be suicidal, or unable to judge distance. Probably this kind of public violence, it had to happen to keep the rest of the prairie dogs on their toes.

The same with hawks or coyotes, right? You can have fear of them born into you, just coursing through as instinct, and you can listen to all the lore circulating around whatever passes for a campfire underground. Every now and again, though, a population needs an object lesson.

This was that lesson.

By crushing this prairie dog under wheel, Trevor was actually saving the lives of countless more, who would learn from this day.

Had he been thinking ahead, he would have gone to the costume store, rented some big fabulous wings, and maybe bought a rubber dog head to pull over his own, so as to drive *three* scares at home at the same time—bikes, birds, canines—but you can't do everything for everyone.

At least he had now successfully put this particular prairie dog out of its self-imposed misery. And—Trevor leaned forward over the bars as he walked slowly backwards—he hadn't even got anything wet on the tread of his tire.

This was a win-win, pretty much.

To say nothing of whatever lucky scavenger was going to find this feast in an hour or two. Surely the flies had already sent up the alert in whatever chemical or buzzy way they had, and were massing this direction to spawn their shiny white young.

"You're welcome," Trevor said to everything that was going to benefit from this.

The prairie dogs just stared at him from their holes.

The way Trevor had always imagined them, they each had small stepladders down there to stand on, that they folded up and tucked away whenever anyone came sniffing.

Such is the animal kingdom, Trevor figured. A whole species of rat standing in line at the hardware store, each with a new ladder tucked under its arm.

He hauled his bike around grandly, like a twelve-year-old making a statement about how fast he was about to go, and he had one foot hiked up on the pedal for the blast downhill when a flicker of motion to his left brought his head around.

It was that prairie dog. The dead one.

It had just shaken, or quivered, or trembled.

Death rattle? Was that a real thing or a movie thing?

Trevor stared the small body down, daring it to move again.

When it didn't, he nodded—the world *could* make sense, if you gave it time—set his right foot on that same pedal, his hands fixed to both grips, and the exact instant he started to roll away, every inquisitive brown face jerked down into their holes all at once, together, as if every one of their stepladders had folded at the same instant.

Every face except for one.

"You too," Trevor said, bouncing his front tire in a way he thought would surely be terrifying to a prairie dog, especially considering what that tire had just done.

The prairie dog didn't flinch.

It wasn't taking any note of Trevor at all.

What it was staring at, it was the dead prairie dog on the concrete path.

Trevor tracked along the sightline between this living prairie dog and the dead one, and finally he nodded, said, "Y'all were together, weren't you?"

As in, mated for life.

As in, just go get one more cheekful of seedheads, okay? I'll stay here and—Trevor didn't know—do something around the den that needs doing.

But no seedheads were coming back, were there?

Worse, no significant other was coming back.

Even worse than *that*, if this prairie dog left behind, whom Trevor had already decided was female, if she stayed there watching like that, she was going to have to see her dead husband first coated in flies, then carried off in the jaws of some impossibly tall animal.

"Just go home," Trevor said to her, bouncing his front tire again.

She didn't.

Her heart was breaking, after all. Your self-preservation instincts, they go away at moments like that, don't they?

For an accidental moment—by rule, he wasn't sentimental, wasn't prone to romantic fits—Trevor looked ahead of him. Down the hill, along the path, two miles ahead. To Belinda.

No way was *she* standing on the porch right now, her hands grasping the top rails, her hair lifting slightly in the wind, her eyes set on all the specks on the horizon that might become her boyfriend.

No way.

But she *was* waiting for this laptop. Maybe even anxiously waiting. Walking across and across her apartment's living room, then executing a neat flip-turn when there was no more carpet to wear down.

And that was kind of the same, wasn't it?

For her intents and purposes, "laptop" and "Trevor" were a single object. The former was part and parcel of the latter. A single, rolling package.

Another way to look at it, Trevor had to allow, was that he was the wrapping, to be discarded once Belinda had the laptop in hand.

Could he have fixed it such that he wouldn't be required to fiddle with it every few days?

He hadn't even considered that.

Or, until he'd topped the hill he was now stranded on the downslope of, he hadn't considered it. But, for a moment up there, that little bit of stillness you get right at the top—hadn't he?

And then he'd been interrupted by a suicidal prairie dog. By a death-penalty prairie dog. By a cautionary-tale prairie dog.

One Little Miss Prairie Dog couldn't seem to pull her black eyes from.

"*He's gone,*" Trevor called across to her, then checked the path behind him, for who might have heard him consoling a stupid prairie dog who probably didn't even register loss or feelings or regret.

All of which Trevor was feeling, as the moment continued swelling.

He'd *lost* time for this soft little speed bump. He *regretted* coming this way instead of the bike lane up on the road, which was actually more direct. He *felt*...what he felt, he supposed, it was some variation of impatience. Almost anger, even.

When he showed up late with the laptop, instead of getting rewarded for having salvaged it, he was going to get questioned about where he'd been. What had taken him so long. Didn't he know her slideshow had to be prepped by *morning*?

No dead prairie dog was going to save him from that. Even if he scraped it up from the concrete, tied it to his rack, led a plume of flies all the way to Belinda's door *and* had a line of car drivers lined up behind him, each ready to recount Trevor's heroics as they'd witnessed them: it had either been the prairie dog or the laptop, ma'am. The rodent or your job. So your boyfriend here, yeah, he risked his limbs and probably his life—his soul too, if killing useless animals counted against you in any way—to make this very special delivery.

Trevor glared across at this prairie dog-in-mourning.

In for a little, in for it all, right?

He laid his bike over gently, then settled the messenger bag down across the frame.

The prairie dog never looked away from her dead husband or brother or father or whatever.

As far as she was concerned, the world had already exploded.

Anything else that happened, it would just be the last few features of the landscape, crumbling over. Still, when Trevor stiff-legged it over to her, he kept out of what he figured would be her peripheral vision.

At the last moment, when he was mid-air, leading with his open hand, his shadow darkening as he fell into it, she did at last turn to him, and—and it was less like she folded down into the hole. More like she was *sucked* down into it.

Trevor's fingers were long and graspy, though. You don't code for seventy-two-hours straight three or four times a month and not get those tendons loose, those muscles tight, those responses automatic.

He latched onto what felt like a hind leg, and snatched her out into the daylight.

The first thing she did was curl up, plant her rodent teeth into the meat around the ball of Trevor's thumb.

The second thing she did was claw a furrow into his wrist with her other hind leg.

The third thing she did was emit some alarm call, like a strangled squeak.

It made Trevor wish once more he had those costume wings on. And that dog head.

He would have squawked back to her from his dog mouth, he was pretty sure. And then come in with the rubber teeth.

Her heart would surely have stopped.

Unlike now, when it was a machine gun pulsing against his palm.

Trevor's left hand came around all on its own, had this prairie dog around the fleshy-but-firm middle from the *back*, so he could extract his other hand from those teeth and claws.

What he almost did was spike her down against the packed earth, to stun her. At which point he might go ahead and just step on her. Not fast, not a stomp, but slow, so she could feel it coming, so she could feel all her blood and internal organs being squeezed up from her middle to her top, to the prairie dog geyser she was about to erupt into.

But she'd bitten him.

That would be too nice.

Trevor stood awkwardly, held her up in victory for all the other prairie dogs to see.

They weren't standing on their little stepladders watching him with their stupid innocent faces, but Trevor knew they were watching. Just, from the safety of their holes—with some crude periscope apparatus, probably.

Watch this, he said, inside.

He strode across the prairie dog town, his eyes set on his bike.

To…what?

He wasn't sure yet.

But something.

Maybe four steps closer to the path, though, his left foot stabbed into a crumbly prairie dog hole, and the rest of him vaulted forward.

The prairie dog went flying.

She hit with a solid splat on the concrete, and rolled.

Trevor, quite aware he was falling and that there was nothing to be done about that, tracked her the whole way.

He brought his foot up from the hole almost in the same motion he'd stabbed it into the hole, and he shambled the rest of the way to the path, dove onto the scurrying prairie dog, first by her tiny hind foot, then, with his bleeding hand, around her middle again.

Something snapped wetly inside her.

She wasn't biting anymore.

Her breath was strained.

Trevor drew her up to his face, said, "You were just going to mope around and die from sadness. This will be better."

It was for her own good, what he had planned.

He was saving her from days or weeks of dealing with the loss of her—*whatever* that other prairie dog had been to her.

Kind to the bitter end, right?

Right, Trevor told himself.

Maybe even a hero, for trading in some piece of himself to keep this prairie dog from all the pain and mental anguish that would precede her death, a death surely eventuated by her not scurrying fast enough from this hole to that one, because she was weighed down by all this rodent sadness, this prairie dog malaise.

Better she go this way.

Better that Trevor was here, yes.

His first thought, the one that blipped up before he could police it, was to open Belinda's laptop, crush this prairie dog between the keyboard and screen. But he'd just end up having to fix it all over again. The laptop.

So.

His bike, it was already on its side.

"That'll work," he said to her.

The prairie dog's small head, it nestled right into that V of space between the chain ring and the chain. On the upside, of course. The intake.

"I don't really have time for this," he said to her, and, with his other hand, pushed the pedal forward.

First the skin of her neck drew up under the greasy links, and then some muscle, some meat.

It wasn't fast.

Chains, they're already and always tight. There's no room in there for the neck and shoulder and head of even a small rodent.

Finally Trevor had to sit on the ground, try to pedal with his actual foot.

The bike just slid forward.

"Well then," he said, and stood the bike up again, stepped into the saddle, the prairie dog's rump hanging there, brushing his ankle. Eyes straight forward, he pedaled ahead with all his weight.

Her head squelched off, fell onto the toe of his left shoe.

Trevor flicked it off.

The body was still connected by skin to the chain, though.

It rode back into the cogs and the hub and the rear shifter, was already there before Trevor could find the brakes.

He threw the bike onto its side, set a foot on the spokes and pulled at the body.

It came away easy.

He spun it as far as he could across the prairie dog town. Far enough that he didn't even hear it land.

Now his hub, and all those little red teeth around it—when Trevor came out from Belinda's, so she could finish her slideshow, his whole back wheel was going to be shiny with flies. He knew it.

He was starting to hate this day.

Try to do one nice thing, and the rest goes straight to hell.

The cars just kept sweeping past.

No other bikers crested the hill. None were climbing from the other way either.

Trevor narrowed his eyes into the distance, trying to

backtrack through all the variables that had spit him out here, instead of already at Belinda's.

It was the laptop, wasn't it?

He couldn't blame the prairie dogs, finally.

Prairie dogs are just stupid animals.

That one he'd just mercy-killed, even, he had probably been just dreaming that it had been in mourning. Probably it was the one that had been elected to watch the horizon for hawks or coyotes, or listen for bikes.

It didn't matter.

One less prairie dog wasn't going to fundamentally unbalance the world, was it?

Trevor chuckled, imagining an existence that fragile.

Which didn't mean he didn't sometimes peel back through pages of code to find one unclosed bracket that was keeping everything from iterating forward.

"One unclosed bracket," he muttered, reeling his eyes in from the distance, focusing them again onto this field of holes.

This was conditional, what he was thinking. A big "if."

But, say that prairie dog he'd just beheaded, what if it *had* been a female? Not necessarily the wife of the one he'd run over—run over *twice*, he guessed, ha—but just a female.

There had to be a fifty percent chance of that, right?

And—and, prairie dogs. They're forever getting snatched up. By hawks. By dogs and coyotes. By cars. By ferrets let loose upon the unsuspecting world.

Everything wants a bite of prairie dog, doesn't it? They're

nature's bite-sized morsels. Their skin isn't skins much as a pouch to hold all their tasty meat.

The only way to fight this, to keep the species happening, that would be for all the females in the town to always be having cycles and cycles of pups, right?

Right.

Meaning, if that *had* been a female he'd cut the head off of, then she surely had some pups down there, already snuffling around blind for their next feeding.

"It never ends," Trevor said, and walked back out into the field. For the body he'd thrown.

No reason to go digging if it had been male, right?

He finally found the small body in the tall grass at the fence.

The ragged stump of a neck was already congealing black. There was grit and blades of dead grass sticking in it.

Trevor didn't care. He spread the hind legs.

Female. Not that he was a prairie dog expert, but from what he could tell, she probably did have a litter down there. A litter starving now.

Trevor dropped the prairie dog, walked from hole to hole until he found the one his foot had stabbed down into, its lips all exploded out from his shoe pulling out.

From that one, he walked back, found the other hole, the one with raw gashes at the lip, from his arm reaching in.

Still no bikes coming up or down the path.

Had he ever been this alone out here? Where was the rest of the world?

It didn't matter.

Using his heel, Trevor crashed the edges of the hole in.

It was easier than he'd figured it would be.

Then he had to get down on his knees, to *tump* the big dry clumps out.

Inside five minutes, he was down into the smelly parts of the den. Where the prairie dogs really *lived*, he guessed.

Then it was just a matter of lying on his side, reaching into this blackness and that blackness, keeping his lips tight so none of the dirt would stick to his teeth. Or, so no *more* of it would. Assuming that even was dirt. Please let it be dirt, Trevor prayed. Please please please.

Finally something back there nibbled at his fingertip.

No, not nibbled: *suckled*.

He withdrew his arm, widened the hole, reached deeper.

He came out with three pups in a single pull.

They were like…his first thought was novelty hacky sacks, maybe. Hacky sacks with stubby little legs. But they were also like pie dough rolled into gummy oblongs and left on the counter until a skin formed.

Mostly they looked like, yes, they *were* going to have been full-on prairie dogs someday.

If their stupid father hadn't darted out into the path of certain death.

If their mother hadn't pined for him for a few breaths too long.

They each had, though. Which meant that the other prairie dogs were just going to leave these pups to starve in the darkness, now.

It was better this way.

Trevor dropped them onto the packed dirt, spacing them out, then, breathing in like that could keep the small wet crunches from coming up through the soles of shoes, he stepped from pup to pup, giving each his full, slow weight.

They didn't know to squeal any alarm cries. The second and third one, they maybe had a flash of recognition—a taste in the air, of the insides of one of them being suddenly on the outside—but Trevor didn't think they had the cognitive gears to ride that smell into recognition, or anticipation.

When you're that young, every new taste, each new smell, it's just one more thing to catalogue, to taste, to make a world from. And then a brief coolness comes, a shade and a pressure, and a sound that, instead of coming at you through the air, comes up through your own soft bones.

And then nothing. Simple as that.

Trevor breathed out, looked around.

Nothing was watching him.

He nodded to himself that this was over, this was it, he was done with this little roadside non-attraction, thank you. He'd done all the good deeds that were in him to do for a single day.

It wasn't going to get him any credit with Belinda, but— he'd heard this once, hadn't he?—you don't do a thing for recognition. You do it because it's the right thing to do.

As far as he was concerned, there had been exactly one single moment of decision: when he'd elected not to endanger Belinda's mostly-repaired laptop. When he'd elected instead to let this suicidal prairie dog take its chances.

The moment the tread of his front tire rolled into the short wiry hair on the left side of that prairie dog, that was actually the moment that whole little prairie dog family had doomed itself.

Trevor had just been a function, here. Not a cause. Not the instigator. Just the one who'd had no choice but to follow through.

Really, the prairie dogs had been lucky it had been him here today, not some other commuter, one without the stomach or the nerve to follow through.

Anyone else riding by, they wouldn't have gotten their hands dirty with all this, would they have?

No way they would have. Zero chance.

It had to be Trevor.

This time on his way through the prairie dog town, back to the path, he wove among the holes. Because he didn't want to start anything else.

He was just shy of the path when a motion to his left flickered in his peripheral, exactly like a short stubby tail, saying something too fast for him to catch, and, he supposed, in a language he didn't exactly know, too.

Trevor closed his eyes, promised himself that if this was that first prairie dog, if it had gasped another breath in, was pulling itself ahead on the one paw that could still reach—

He opened his eyes.

It wasn't that dead prairie dog.

It was a living one.

Just watching him.

"What?" Trevor said.

The prairie dog just stared.

And it wasn't alone, was it?

Trevor laughed to himself, looking from face to face, hole to hole. The whole town was up again, tracking him.

"You're welcome," Trevor said, affecting a little bow, and shuffled forward under the weight of all this adulation.

The prairie dogs all came down off their stepladders as one, were gone.

All except…how many was this?

Four. No, five.

"Tough guys, yeah?" Trevor said, then hopped up onto one foot, so he could see the bottom of his left shoe.

The tread was packed with infant prairie dog and bloodied dirt.

Still hopping, he held that sole out to these five tough guys.

They didn't look at his shoe at all, but past it, at Trevor.

No, into Trevor.

"Screw this," Trevor said, and stepped forward, planning to go right across the one of these five between him and the path.

At the last moment, though, he couldn't, irrationally sure that the reason there was five prairie dogs, not four, not six, was that these weren't animal heads, but faces painted onto the fingers of a giant hand, one he was standing in the palm of.

"Ha ha very funny," he said, stepping along the path instead of onto it.

Of course there was another hole where he planned to gain the concrete again.

Of course another head popped up there.

Trevor looked back to the other five, but they were gone.

"Where'd all your friends—" he said, but swallowed it.

The other *four* were there again, spaced...not quite evenly around him. But definitely in an arc between him and the path. Him and his bike. Him and escape.

Which is to say: a guy who could fix a laptop over three consecutive nights, a guy who could walk across baby prairie dogs, each step bringing death, a guy who, for all intents and most purposes, was the real and true god of all these low things, he was scared of...what, exactly?

Being watched? By *prairie dogs*?

Belinda would love this part of the story, he knew.

Which was precisely why he wasn't going to be sharing it.

Again, he looked up and down the path, for witnesses.

No one.

It was like he'd pedaled through some invisible aperture, into a side-world. No, it was like he was between places.

In this one, he was the only commuter out at two-thirty on a Thursday afternoon.

Maybe everyone who slammed down this hill, they rode though this same non-place, just, it looked exactly the same as the reality they knew, so they just rode right back out.

Except—except this time, *this* day, Trevor had stopped, hadn't he?

For a stupid prairie dog.

"Screw this," he said to this world, "I'm going home," and found his muscles all tensing, for this step he was about to take across the one prairie dog between him and the concrete.

There was just a hole there now, though.

"That's right," Trevor said, liking the way it sounded coming out—like he was in a movie, like he was the star of that movie—and, swinging his foot across for the concrete, he leaned over maybe ten degrees, for a better angle down into the hole.

Just to see if that prairie dog was tucked away, waiting for him to be a safe enough distance away. Just to see the last foot of that stepladder he knew had to have just been there.

What he saw instead was…wetness?

A little pool down there?

No, not a pool. Pools don't bulge up.

And this, it wouldn't be water, either. It was too black.

Trevor leaned down, fully aware that there was no chance in hell of him sticking a hand down there to investigate. But he could look closer, anyway. He had one foot still on the concrete, firmly in and on the undeniably-real world. It's not like anything could happen.

The wetness, then—this was the only possible word for it—it *blinked*.

Trevor sucked air in hard enough that his throat closed.

Now there was just that bulging black shine again.

But—but if that *had* been a blink. If it had, then the lid, the eyelid, it had been the color of the packed-down dirt, hadn't it?

The color of prairie dog.

Trevor shook his head no, that this was too stupid. That

of course he would see something like this, after having just done what he'd had to do.

To prove it, he gave that particular hole a wide berth, and walked along the path three steps, to the next hole. This one was farther out from the concrete.

Trevor put one foot down onto the dirt by the hole, gave it his weight like testing to be sure it would hold, and then he took the last step, the one that got him the angle he needed to look down into that blackness.

This time he caught one of them napping, it looked like.

Instead of a giant eyeball in this hole, there was that dry brown hair.

"Big boy," Trevor said, about how this prairie dog spread out when lying down.

At which point that prairie dog flicked up, became another enormous eyelid.

In that huge deep marble of an eye, a pupil dilated, taking Trevor in.

He laughed. It was the only response that made any kind of sense whatsoever.

"So, so," he said, still not believing this. "If you're an eye"—this hole—"and *you're* an eye"—the first hole—"then, then, then the *mouth* would either be…"

Trevor turned to look behind him, to the path.

"It would either be under the concrete," he said, like a dare, "or it would be—"

Trevor visually spaced the two "eye"-holes, then centered himself, stepped back grandly, planted both feet.

"—here," he said.

And he chuckled. He was *hoping* someone would pedal past, now. Just so he could *try* to explain.

There's this giant prairie dog under the ground, he would tell them, then jump once right where he was standing. *Right here. Just lying face-up.*

At first they probably wouldn't smile, not sure how to take Trevor's claim.

Then they would risk one corner of their mouth rising, in what could either be a smile or the first part of whatever excuse they were going to extricate themselves with.

Trevor would just shrug, let the awkwardness balloon around them both, like they were going to ride away in it.

He tried that exact shrug out—his left shoulder, like usual—and that was when the ground opened up beneath him, into a maw.

A prairie dog's teeth are curled in, like most rodents'.

It's so their prey—seeds, vegetable matter—can't escape, can only be pulled in.

But some are hungrier than that.

Trevor went in feet first, the dirt clods around him already bubbling with his own blood.

"No, this isn't—!" he screamed, but there was no on there to hear.

The earth he tried to dig into with his hands was falling in with him, and there were fast cracks running from hole to hole, from the pressure pushing up under this crust of earth.

Forty or fifty feet down the hill—not the path, but the

packed-dirt slope leading to the fence—a long black claw speared up from a hole. The hind feet were gripping while the mouth pulled.

Trevor was gone almost instantly.

By the time the next bike sweeps past, the churned earth marking his passage is already starting to congeal in the sun.

Two days later, the rain comes softly, rounding off the hard edges of the upturned clods, and then the sun bakes it beyond suspicion.

Over the next couple of weeks, the bike lying now alongside the path loses first its canvas messenger bag, then its wheels and tires, and then one morning the frame is bent, from whatever kids had been walking past after dark.

On the third week a woman walks alone up the concrete path, and stops at the bent frame of this weathered bicycle.

Does she recognize it?

She does stop, lower herself to it. Run her hand along the frame, the forks. The grips on the handlebars, as if the palm of her hand can remember what her eyes can't.

"Trev?" she says, because there's no one close enough to hear.

No one human, anyway.

Standing up from one hole on the other side of the path, a new prairie dog is watching her.

Because just its upper body is aboveground, she can't see its tail flicking back and forth, hesitantly, as if not wanting to believe this.

Because her ears aren't tuned for the sound, she doesn't hear the mewling whine in its throat.

She stands, looks behind her for anyone coming up the path. When no one is, she fingerwaves bye to this cute little doll of a creature, then turns uphill, for the rest of this path.

She looks back, of course.

Not because she's particularly fond of rodents, but because this one seems intent in a way she wouldn't have ascribed to a prairie dog. Like it's trying to tell her something?

She finally shakes her head no, that whatever she'd been thinking, it was stupid, and right when she turns uphill again, the racing bike crests from the other direction, slams down towards her all at once, the rider's head down because his legs are pumping, pumping, pumping.

The impact of helmet-on-face is brutal. It splits the afternoon in two, and releases pungent new smells into it.

Afterward, she lies there panting on the concrete, her breath hitching slower and slower, her blood pooling under her cheek, using a crack in the concrete as a channel.

The cyclist is rolling like an injured log through the prairie dog town, careless of the holes or the dusk caking into his sweat.

Slowly, taking care to fold his stepladder, the lone prairie dog withdraws, crawls back into the darkest, most remote part of its new den.

With its nose pressed tight into the corner, all it can smell for moments at a time is loamy wetness, cloying soil, damp decay.

It breathes deep, trying to fill its whole head with just that.

BIOGRAPHIES AND ENDNOTES

Kristi DeMeester is the author of *Such a Pretty Smile, Beneath,* and the short fiction collection *Everything That's Underneath.* Her short stories have appeared in *Black Static, The Dark,* among others, and she's had stories included in several volumes of Ellen Datlow's *The Best Horror of the Year, Year's Best Weird Fiction,* and Stephen Jones' *Best New Horror.* She is at work on her next novel. Find her online at www.kristidemeester.com.

"Slipping Petals from Their Skins"—I wanted to write about the connection between sisters. About faith and resurrection. About the lengths girls are encouraged to go to be considered beautiful. All mixed together with my childhood obsession with Cicely Mary Barker's flower fairies. This was the story that came out.

Kate Dollarhyde is a Nebula and GLAAD Media Award-winning game designer and writer of speculative fiction. Her short stories have been published in *Fireside Fiction, Lackington's, Beneath Ceaseless Skies,* and other magazines. Previously, she was the co-editor-in-chief of the speculative fiction magazine *Strange Horizons*. She was also a narrative designer at Obsidian Entertainment, where she wrote for *The Outer Worlds*, the *Pillars of Eternity* series, and *Pentiment*. She lives in California.

"The Arrow of Time"—After another terrible fire season in California, I found myself divided by competing impulses—a desperate desire to return to a time before I understood what our climate change-ravaged future held, and an anxious need to begin planning for how to meet that future when it inevitably arrived. I knew I wasn't alone in these divisions, and so in writing "The Arrow of Time," I wondered, what did these obsessions offer us? What kinds of people could these impulses lead us to become? And, ultimately, how could our future selves survive the world our past had made?

Brian Evenson is the author of a dozen and a half books of fiction, most recently *The Glassy, Burning Floor of Hell*. His story collection *Song for the Unraveling of the World* won the Shirley Jackson Award and the World Fantasy Award and was a finalist for the Ray Bradbury Prize. He lives in Los Angeles and teaches at CalArts.

"Garnier"—Though I'm best known as a writer of literary horror, I've long been interested in roman noir and detective fiction, which I read almost obsessively (indeed, the title of the story is a nod to Pascal Garnier, a French noir novelist I admire). Usually I end up mixing noir with some other genre, curious to see, for instance, what happens if noir and SF collide (as in my novel *Immobility*) or what happens when noir takes on some of the trappings of religious horror (*Last Days*). But "Garnier" is straight-ahead noir—my attempt to see if I can write something that feels a little bit like Patricia Highsmith's *The Cry of the Owl* but nevertheless still like me. «Garnier» offers two voices, one of the husband whose wife has vanished, and the other of the man in love with this wife, and allows each, in turn, to offer their version of the events.

KURT FAWVER is a writer of horror, weird fiction, and literature that oozes between the cracks of genre. His stories have been collected in three books—*Forever, in Pieces, The Dissolution of Small Worlds*, and *We are Happy, We are Doomed*. His work has also won a Shirley Jackson Award and been nominated for the Bram Stoker Award. Kurt holds a PhD in literature and teaches writing classes at several colleges. He's glad to be a part of your literary world.

About the story: I wanted to write a story in the vein of Thomas Ligotti meets Steven Millhauser—something desperately pessimistic but also socially aware, decaying and otherworldly yet tracing the border of quaint normalcy. I also wanted to write about cosmic clowns and cancer, which seemed to fit those two writers' sensibilities. "Etch the Unthinkable" is what emerged when I threw all those elements in a pot and stirred.

MICHELLE GOLDSMITH is a Melbourne-based author and science communicator, whose fiction often inhabits the shady borderlands between genres. Her short fiction has appeared in various publications both within Australia and overseas, and she's been short-listed for both the Aurealis Award and the Ditmar Award.

I wrote "Love Story; an Exorcism" after a discussion about disturbing stories that explore taboo topics without resorting to gratuity. Unhealthy and abusive friendships between children are rarely talked about, though I've known multiple people who've experienced them. In some ways, the story itself is intentionally dissatisfying. The protagonist will never get a satisfactory explanation for what happened. They're still trapped in the perspective of the child they were, guessing at answers and basically attempting to build a complete picture from too few pieces. In the same way, the reader doesn't get a single definitive answer about the story's ending. They'll just have to deal without real closure. It's definitely not a story for everyone, but it felt like it was still worth telling.

BIOGRAPHIES AND ENDNOTES

MARIA HASKINS is a Swedish-Canadian writer and reviewer of speculative fiction. She lives just outside Vancouver with a husband, two children, several birds, a snake, and a very large black dog. Her latest short story collection *Wolves & Girls* is now out from Brain Jar Press. Maria›s work has appeared in her 2021 short story collection *Six Dreams About the Train*, and also in *The Best Horror of the Year Volume 13*, *Black Static*, *Interzone*, *The Deadlands*, *Fireside*, *Beneath Ceaseless Skies*, *Flash Fiction Online*, *Strange Horizons*, *Cast of Wonders*, *PseudoPod*, *Escape Pod*, *Podcastle*, *Diabolical Plots*, *Kaleidotrope*, and elsewhere. Find out more on her website mariahaskins.com.

"Metal, Sex, Monsters"—The working title for this story was "Eat Me Alive" which is a track from Judas Priest's album *Defenders of the Faith* and if you listen to it, I think you'll get the inspiration. I did feel like that title was a bit on the nose, and even a bit spoilery, so I came up with "Metal, Sex, Monsters," a title which could also describe most of Judas Priest's oeuvre. I finished this story, submitted it to *Gamut*, and got an acceptance two days later. It was my first pro-sale and still one of the highlights of my writing career.

STEPHEN GRAHAM JONES is the NYT bestselling author of some thirty novels and collections, and there's some novellas and comic books in there as well. Most recent are *Don't Fear* the Reaper and the ongoing *Earthdivers*. Up before too long are *The Angel of Indian Lake* and *I Was a Teenage Slasher*. Stephen lives and teaches in Boulder, Colorado.

"The God of Low Things"—I'm always on my mountain bike, here in Boulder. And I'm always cruising through some prairie dog town, hoping these little dudes will dart out of the way, please. But I'm always worried what if one of them doesn't make it out from under my tire, right? I mean, I'd feel terrible, of course, but, too, what cycle of justice might this open me up to? Imaging consequences like this is kind of my way of making me slow down when the prairie dogs are scurrying back and forth across the path. It's their town, not mine, and therefore it's on me to tread carefully, to not just trounce through like Godzilla. If I don't, I mean, then a Godzilla might rise to settle the score

---

Stories by KATE JONEZ have been nominated three times for the Bram Stoker Award and once for The Shirley Jackson Award. Her short fiction has appeared in *The Best Horror of the Year, Black Static, Pseudopod, Gamut* and *Haunted Nights* edited by Ellen Datlow and Lisa Morton. She is currently working on a series of interactive stories. Watch her progress on Instagram: @K8jonez and Youtube: @KateJonez.

"The Moments Between"—The inspiration for this story comes from an idea I've pondered for a while. I wanted to explore what happens after the main events? Is it possible to tell a story set in liminal spaces? In this story, the horror that confronts a mother is too intense to face head on. Turns out there's a lot going on in the aftermath.

CASSANDRA KHAW is the *USA Today* bestselling author of *Nothing But Blackened Teeth* and the Bram Stoker Award-winner, *Breakable Things*. Other notable works of theirs are *The Salt Grows Heavy* and British Fantasy Award and Locus Award finalist, *Hammers on Bone*. Khaw's work can be found in places like *The Magazine of Fantasy & Science Fiction*, *Year's Best Science Fiction and Fantasy*, and *Tor.com*. Khaw is also the co-author of *The Dead Take the A Train*, co-written with bestselling author Richard Kadrey.

"The Ghost Stories We Tell Around Photon Fires "—I wrote this story as I was grappling with the idea of surviving our lovers, how to proceed when there's such an enormous absence. Would I live in a loop if it meant more time with the one I lost? Yes. Would I subject others to purgatory to stay with the love lost? Also yes. (This story is also about the flip side, about helping our loved ones let go, about letting go, about letting the story continue.)

DR. HELEN MARSHALL is a Senior Lecturer of Creative Writing at the University of Queensland. She has won the

World Fantasy Award, the British Fantasy Award and the Shirley Jackson Award for her two collections of Weird short stories. Her debut novel, *The Migration*, argued for the need to remain hopeful, even in the worst circumstances. It was one of *The Guardian's* top science fiction books of the year. She directs the WhatIF Lab at the University of Queensland, which specialises in creative arts, speculative fiction and imagination-led workshops for researchers from different backgrounds and disciplines.

"They Are Passing By Without Turning"—I wrote this story after a research trip to Prague and other parts of eastern Europe in 2015. I was fascinated by the idea of exploring what happens in the margins of stories, the way the great Gothic manuscripts of the Middle Ages crawl with dragons and devils and grotesques of an even stranger kind. A young woman becomes swept up in the politics of her age—but we don't see her rise to power or even her fall, just the often clumsy attempts to make sense of the absurdity of human affairs.

KATHRYN E. MCGEE's stories and poems have appeared in Kelp Journal, Ladies of the Fright, Scoundrel Time, Gamut Magazine, Horror Library Vol. 6, and the Bram Stoker Award-nominated Chromophobia anthology. She has an MFA from UC Riverside Palm Desert and is an Active Member of the Horror Writers Association. Please visit www.kathrynemcgee.com.

"The Mark" is about anxiety and mounting dread, my two favorite subjects. It's meant to capture the nervous vibes of a first date and the monstrous feeling of losing control. I used body horror to tell this story because romantic outings are personal, maybe fleshy, encounters and there's nothing worse that something going wrong with our body when we're feeling insecure.

ERIC REITAN's award-winning short fiction has appeared in numerous magazines and anthologies, including *The Magazine of Fantasy and Science Fiction, Deciduous Tales, Tiferet Journal,* and the *Alien Invasions* and *Weird Horror* anthologies from Flame Tree Press. He is also the author of three non-fiction books and dozens of academic and public-facing articles on religion, ethics, and philosophy. When he isn't writing or playing his violin, he teaches philosophy at Oklahoma State University.

I used to facilitate prison workshops—immersive weekend workshops aimed at teaching conflict resolution skills and cultivating a spirit of nonviolence. Participants often shared experiences that posed roadblocks to a more nonviolent future, including accounts of traumatic abuse. One inmate shared her attempts to shield her little brother from her mother's brutal boyfriend, and her narrative was so vivid it haunted me for weeks. I kept imagining myself as that little brother—a boy whose only hope came from a girl not much older than him. "The Bubblegum Man" was born from those imaginings.

JAN STINCHCOMB is the author of *Verushka* (JournalStone), *The Kelping* (Unnerving), *The Blood Trail* (Red Bird Chapbooks) and *Find the Girl* (Main Street Rag). Her stories have appeared in *Bourbon Penn*, *The Horror Is Us* (Mason Jar Press) and *Menacing Hedge*, among other places. A Pushcart nominee, she is featured in *Best Microfiction 2020* and *The Best Small Fictions 2018 & 2021*. She lives in Southern California with her family and is an associate fiction editor for *Atticus Review*. Find her at janstinchcomb.com; Twitter: @janstinchcomb; Instagram: @jan_stinchcomb.

"Cradle Lake"—Absent parents are the key to this story—with the parents out of the way, the kids can get to work. I first encountered parentless (or at least motherless) children in the fairy tales, my earliest and most constant source of literary inspiration. The kids here take ordinary objects, plastic baby dolls, and imbue them with magic. They create a surprisingly peaceful world, based on their values, which puts traditional authority to shame. I think this story remains relevant because parenting is always being scrutinized and found to come up short.

E. CATHERINE TOBLER's short fiction has appeared in *Clarkesworld*, *F&SF*, *Beneath Ceaseless Skies*, *Apex Magazine*, and others. Her novella, *The Necessity of Stars*, from Neon

Hemlock, was a finalist for the Nebula, Utopia, and Sturgeon Awards. She currently edits *The Deadlands*.

"Figure 8"—One random evening I was in conversation with a friend—who knows what we were actually talking about, but what my brain retained was a question: "What happened to all the Ripleys?" (*Alien Resurrection*) Fire, sure, but my brain went another route, where clones lived and had lives, as broken as they may be, and didn't necessarily want to be found by another of the clones, even if they remembered them all. That's where "Figure 8" came from. The choice of 8 was deliberate, as 8 is also an infinity symbol standing up on its end.

RICHARD THOMAS edited *Gamut* magazine and Dark House Press, as well as four anthologies—*Burnt Tongues* (with Chuck Palahniuk and Dennis Widmyer), *The New Black, The Lineup: 20 Provocative Women Writers,* and *Exigencies*. He is the award-winning author of nine books: four novels—*Incarnate, Breaker, Disintegration,* and *Transubstantiate*; four collections—*Spontaneous Human Combustion, Tribulations, Staring Into the Abyss,* and *Herniated Roots*; and one novella of *The Soul Standard*. He has been nominated for the Bram Stoker (twice), Shirley Jackson, Thriller, and Audie awards. Visit www.storyvilleonline.com and www.whatdoesnotkillme.com for more information.

MICHAEL WEHUNT is a semi-reclusive creature living in the trees of Atlanta with his partner and their dog. Together, they hold the horrors at bay. He is the author of the collections *Greener Pastures* and *The Inconsolables*, and his debut novel, *The October Film Haunt*, is forthcoming from St. Martin's Press. His work has been a finalist for the Shirley Jackson Award, shortlisted for the International Association for the Fantastic in the Arts' Crawford Award, and published in Spain, where it garnered nominations for the Premio Ignotus and Premio Amaltea, winning the latter. Find him in the digital woods at www.michaelwehunt.com.

"An Ending (Ascent)"—A premise that wouldn't let me go: What if the human race achieved true immortality—the holy grail—but some were too old to receive it? Those unfortunate ones would have to watch the light in the eyes of those around them, and it would stir up such an existential and profound complexity of emotions. The world would change drastically, too. I wanted to take a long look at that. The reality of this setting might play out in a bleaker way, but if we can't find hope in the future, we might as well give up.

ACKNOWLEDGMENTS

I want to thank everyone that supported the original *Gamut* magazine—the subscribers, patrons, authors, editors, and illustrators. It was a heady experience, and I learned a lot. In fact, because it was such a fulfilling experience, we have re-launched the magazine, and added a publishing house, and teaching academy. We are now the House of Gamut. Special thanks to my editors at *Gamut*—Mercedes Yardley, Dino Parenti, Casey Frechette, and Heather Foster, as well as illustrator Luke Spooner. As we move forward, I have to thank Richard Wood for his partnership, and everyone else that is joining us on this adventure. And as always, I have to thank my family—my wife, Lisa, my children, Ricky and Tyler, as well as my mother, and my brother, Bill. None of this would be possible without a great support system, filled with encouragement and kind words. Onward and upward!

—Richard Thomas

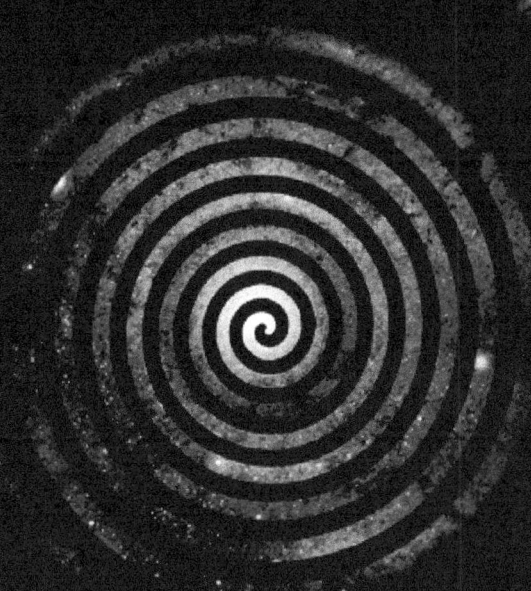